CRIMES
OF WAR

CRIMES
OF WAR

PETER HOGG

THOMAS DUNNE BOOKS
ST. MARTIN'S PRESS ☙ NEW YORK

This is a work of fiction, and the characters in it are solely the creation of the author. Any resemblance to actual persons—with the exception of historical figures—is entirely coincidental. When historical figures consort with fictional characters, the results are, necessarily, fiction. Similarly, some events have been created to serve fictional purposes.

THOMAS DUNNE BOOKS.
An imprint of St. Martin's Press.

www.stmartins.com

ISBN 0-312-26954-4   FIC HOG
$22.95

First published in Canada by McClelland & Stewart Inc.

First U.S. Edition: February 2001

10 9 8 7 6 5 4 3 2 1

To Janet

CHAPTER ONE

I

———

My past is a shallow grave. Beneath a thin layer of soil and filth lies the truth of me. Time has passed and the events of my life have faded to the colour of dust, the dust that settles over will and memory and pain. I once had control over my memories, but now, in the brightness of this morning, I cannot hold them back. They dart in and out of my consciousness like flashes of light or the flickers of passing, furtive shadows, like flecks of light and particles of sound that are all at once there, and gone, and there again.

I once fled from an old world that was used up and broken, but a part of me remained behind in that time and place like a ghost or a secret that haunts dark ruins and bitter landscapes; no matter if the scars have healed on the surface and the patching up is seen to be done. I fled from it, leaving everything and nothing, all at once, escaping shackles or a noose or some other lamentable fate. But the faces and the names remained with me like degrees of varying consciousness. They were my secrets. I kept them close and guarded them, a fetish born of concealment. Lies and subterfuge were essential to my being and I believed that my vigilance had been rewarded. I remained free, but have I remained truly forgotten? Has my face been buried by the years? In the years of my life, Fortune has smiled down upon me, as it does so often on those least deserving of her favour. My name is Friedrich Reile, but that is a secret, too.

Now the past, *my past*, has returned. It came rolled up and stuffed into the tight recesses of my mailbox.

The envelope, stamped and sealed, bore my name and my address typed in black ink on the front. I could see no return address. Inside I found two photographs. The first was of a young man, perhaps barely seventeen, and he wore a black uniform with thick epaulettes, but no insignias could be seen. His face, pale against the darkness of his tunic, was slightly rounded, soft and boyish, his eyes focused on a point just to the side of the camera. There was a trace of a smile on his lips, like a self-conscious smirk, suggesting perhaps that he doubted the underlying seriousness of being photographed.

The second photo, although of the same man, was as much a contrast to the first as it was a complement. Its focus was sharper, with a sepia tone, and although the man was still young, he nevertheless appeared older, without a glimmer remaining of the boy in that face. There was no softness now; the face was thinner, attenuated, sharper, and the lips were closed in a fashion that no longer allowed for any smiles or smirks. The slightly lidded eyes seemed darker now; black, as the uniform he wore was black. Those eyes, *my eyes*, stared straight into the camera, beyond it, in fact, as if the camera had never been there.

The reverse of the first photograph is blank, but on the opposite side of the second photograph there was a date written. *September 1942.* I had not seen those photos in forty-five years.

The past has been delivered to my doorstep.

There is someone who knows me. Someone remembers my name.

The time is now.

I bought a diary today, the kind made of stiff yellowy-white pages enfolded by a cover made of thick woven cloth. I sat in the study of my house near the window, which looked onto my front yard, and I flipped open the front cover, pressing the tip of my pen on that first blank page. I wrote out the date. And so I began my confession:

November 14, 1994.

Between the chaos and the certainty, I watch and wait. I have walked among the dead that lay at my feet in forlorn heaps. I have heard the footsteps that follow mine, and I have seen shadows and figures that hover in the corner of my eye and narrowly escape my gaze. In my old age I am alone, childless, my dear wife gone, ravaged by a disease, obliterated by the indiscriminate operations of Death.

Smells. Sounds. Voices. The sound of crying, of weeping. The hoarse, raw sound of human voices barking orders; the sound of gunfire, sharp and cutting through the raw air of late autumn. A roaring, a silence. *And* I hear the names again, names I had not heard uttered in fifty years: Holtzmann, Richmaier, Nachtigal, Nürnberg, Goertzen, and

Christmann; above all there was Christmann. He has never been forgotten.

For the many years that followed the day I left Germany, my sister continued to write long and loving letters, and in each she would tell me how much she missed me since our mother had died, and how she loved me. She promised one day to come and visit me in my new country. But then the trials began and the letters stopped. Instead, she sent me small packages full of clippings from the journals and newspapers written by all the reporters who had attended the trials. She had carefully cut out each article and pasted them to larger pieces of paper, which she folded in half and wrapped in brown paper. I expect that she read every word. How could she not? I know that my name never appeared in those articles, for I read them closely, searching for even a hint that I had been implicated. Nevertheless, she knew. When the trials were over and the journals and the newspapers moved on to other stories, the packages ceased to arrive.

Years later, after Christmann's conviction, I did receive one last clipping. It recounted how Christmann had been released from prison after serving nine years and had shortly thereafter died. Christmann had been defiant throughout his trial, the article said, and it described how he had even lunged at the police when they'd come to arrest him at his home. By that time he had returned to Germany after having spent several years in Paraguay after the war. The journalist wrote that Christmann had been in a rage when he learned of the reasons for his arrest and for his trial. He would never respect the premise of his trial nor the legitimacy of any court to try him. He held those who purported to judge him in contempt.

"He could not comprehend," the article went on to say, "how following the orders of his superiors could be construed as crimes of war. He had done his duty, he had done the dirty work, but it was the higher-ups, the leaders of his nation, of the status quo, who had given the orders. Where were they now? Safe and sound, or dead, perhaps. He had been held responsible for the crimes of a nation. The proceedings wore him down, especially the realization that he and a handful of individuals would be held accountable for the sins of all the others. He would be the scapegoat for the Beast of collective guilt. This broke him in a way no prison sentence could ever accomplish. He had implemented the orders. What about the men who'd given the orders? And all the others who'd done the shooting, when were they to be tried?"

That article, that fragment, was the last I ever heard from my sister. That was her final message.

I remember him now, his body slim and muscled, his face lean, sharp, precise, as if etched. He had been an athlete before the war, a celebrated skier and Alpiner, and his manner of commanding betrayed a love of games and sport and competition. He was keen and ambitious, but he should have been elsewhere, fighting some other kind of war, not the war of *Aktionen* and "special operations." Had he been somewhere else, in some other place, in some other capacity, I believe that everything would have been different for him. Instead, he was absorbed and polluted by events that weren't necessarily of his choosing. He might otherwise have been a good man. But he was betrayed by others, he was betrayed by circumstance and he was punished for not betraying himself.

I felt as if I'd been struck within, by a thick, hard fist, when I read that last piece. I saw his name and the words that followed in columns on yellowed paper clippings. I did not want to let myself think of him. That was the past and I could not afford to reflect upon it, not when I had made a new start, when I had a wife and a job in a new country that might just as well have been in a different universe. Christmann was the past, and once he was gone nothing could be gained by glancing back in his direction. Still, he did not vanish completely from my mind. My memories of him were stored like so much unopened mail, unfinished business that would never truly go away.

I kept the newspaper clippings in a trunk, and though it's been years since I read them, I can still recall the details. There were several trials and the testimonies of some of the witnesses were reported at great length. Many were rife with denials and half-truths. Every man, it seems, had been an orderly or a guard or a driver or a clerk. Not one had been a shooter, though they had heard of such things. It was never them; it could never have been them. I smiled without joy when I read this and I understood why such men fumbled about with prevarications. I suppose a lie is not a lie if you believe it to be true. I would have done the same. I would have denied the allegations, and after a while I might even have convinced myself that I was truly innocent of such crimes.

There were others, of course; there had to be others.

Without others none of it could have happened. I was there and I know what I did. Yet with the passage of time I came to feel that it was as if someone else had done those things, someone so divorced and remote from the man I became. The truths we face, the truths about ourselves, are bearable once distilled with half-truths and filtered through subtle lies. And of course time may have helped to take away the sting, to inure me to my past. But I wondered now if time was but a delusion and that my past was not so remote after all.

It was not so hard to fool yourself. That was how some men learned to cope. I remember that there was a driver named Brunschen. He was red-headed, as young as I perhaps. It seemed to me, too, that he was always drunk. He had joined the unit when we were stationed in Taganrog, on the Sea of Azov. Previous to that he had been a member of Einsatzkommando 6B. In Taganrog our unit was billeted in a school. The first night he arrived I spoke to him as we sat together in a classroom that now served as a mess hall. In a corner of the room there was a jumbled pile of tiny chairs and tables, most of them upturned and broken, pushed to the side to make room for the long wooden mess tables. The room had once been a kindergarten.

Brunschen spoke to me about the new trucks that had arrived the day before. His voice was low and dry-sounding as he told me that he had been the first to operate one of these vehicles when he was with his former unit in Simferopol. It was rumoured that many of the various kommando officers had begun to complain to their superiors that the assigned tasks were exacting a tremendous physical and mental toll on their men. They argued that something had to be done, and so the trucks were sent for and Brunschen was one of the drivers who delivered them.

"These are special trucks, you understand? They are meant to make our lives easier." Brunschen said.

The room was quiet now and Brunschen and I were the only ones left after dinner. I asked him what he meant, and at first he was reluctant to tell me, but I persuaded him to provide more details.

"How do the trucks work? What does one do to operate them?"

He replied that *he* had *done* nothing. He told me that he had first driven one of the trucks in Simferopol with his former unit. His sergeant had ordered him to sit behind the wheel, and as he waited there he heard a commotion at the rear of the truck. He believed that the noise was of people being loaded through a rear door into the back of the truck, but he could not see what was actually happening. Then the sergeant gave him the key to start the truck. He was ordered to drive along a special route that went out of the city and towards the anti-tank ditches beside the collective farm. There were other men waiting for him at the ditches, but he remained in the truck and heard the sounds of some of the kommando men unloading the back of the truck. They were coughing and spitting, and he heard the sounds of cursing.

"But I saw nothing," he said to me. He was tapping one finger on the rough wooden table as he spoke these words, and his body was bent slightly over to one side as the vodka and schnapps began to get the better of him. The light in the mess hall was dim now and the air was dry and chalky. "You understand that I saw nothing? I stayed behind the wheel of the truck and I did nothing. I simply drove."

Brunschen was correct. These were very special trucks. I saw one of them in use a few days later. Before dawn, I was driven with ten other kommando men to an empty airstrip two kilometres west of Taganrog. It was early spring, so the air was still cold, and in the faint light I could see the empty farm fields that lay on either side of the airstrip. The sky was very clear and the stars and the night were giving way to the pale blue of the morning. We waited at a ditch dug parallel to the airstrip. I had been ordered to assist in the unloading and was filled with dread because I knew by then what to expect. We were issued double rations of schnapps while we waited. I felt the sting of the liquor tear into me as I swallowed, and then a warming, softening sensation followed as the alcohol took effect. Some of the men began to joke with each other, and the tension of that morning was for a moment relieved.

I saw the first truck arrive with Brunschen behind the wheel. The truck stopped short of us and turned to back up to the ditch. It was similar to the transport trucks that the kommando used to move its men and carry out operations, except this truck had been modified, and a large box-like structure had been built on the back, making it resemble a van. It was painted dark grey, with no markings on the front or sides of the cab. An attempt had been made to camouflage the vehicle with sets of wooden shutters fastened to both sides. They had been secured as if opened, revealing false windows with curtains painted on the sides of the truck.

At the rear was a door with a thick metal lever. Baumer, the sergeant, warned us to stay away from the truck when this door was opened. When the truck stopped, Baumer stepped up to the door and yanked the lever. Then he moved back a pace and a great blue and white cloud rushed out, dense as liquid. We waited for the fumes to dissipate and then we were ordered to go inside the truck. The first man to enter the vehicle immediately turned and rushed past me on his way out, one hand pressed hard against his mouth to stem the flow of vomit. He fell to the ground, bent double with heaves and coughs. I remained standing outside at the open door and stared into the shadow that was the back of the truck. I watched as traces of the cloud still hovered momentarily about the twisted, dark forms that lay motionless on the floor of the vehicle. Then the blue and white wisps rose from that darkness and vanished like an exhaled breath that is seen for a moment before being lost in the cold of the night.

A second truck arrived, a smaller version of the first. The driver was a *Volksdeutscher*, like myself, named Sebastien Richmaier. He yelled from the cab, telling us to hurry. Then he promised that the next load would be easier because it would be made up only of children.

Despite what Brunschen had heard, the trucks were not always efficient, and improvements had to be made to the design. A device like a lever was added. It was adjusted with a pair of pliers and allowed the driver to modify and control the flow of carbon monoxide. This was the improvement that had been promised. The shootings had begun to take their toll and so the trucks would now perform the special tasks. But this meant that Brunschen and Richmaier would have to do more than simply drive. They received new instructions in the workings of that tiny lever that would have to be pulled from time to time to ensure that the trucks performed their task. That was the way it was. There was always one more task to perform.

There are names that I can put to faces and I remember the cities and towns. I was at Taganrog and Mariupol and the courtyard in Krasnodar. I remember, too, an empty brown field that gave way to a ravine I followed towards a river. It was summer and the river was framed by a warm haze that drifted slowly and lazily in the still afternoon. The water was textured and dappled, as light and reflections danced on the surface. The burping sounds of the guns faded in the distance and I reached down to splash water at the drying blood that stained my high black boots. My hands still trembled then.

Before any of that happened, I lived in Muntau, a village in the Molotschna German colony in Tokmak district, southern Ukraine. I was born there. My father was a surgeon at the hospital until the Communists took him away in 1937 because he was German. After that, my mother, sister, brother, and I moved to Tokmak, where my mother was a schoolteacher. Four years later the Communists came for my brother and took him away as well, and drafted him into the army. Like my father before him, he too disappeared.

The war made its way to my home.

I heard the sounds of distant thunder and angry rumblings that drew closer every day. One day I felt the ground shake and knew it was not thunder. My mother and my sister were sitting in the kitchen, holding each other's hands, and they called to me to stay inside. But I was too excited and ran out the door and into the street toward the market. There I stood with others in the city and watched ragged columns of Russian soldiers heading east and I knew this meant a retreat. I looked to see if my brother was among them, but I could not see him in that stream of blackened and bloodied faces. The summer air was thick and relentless and it smelled now of blood and death. I saw panic and fear in the eyes of those soldiers. I felt no fear then, and I was happy to see so many Russians fleeing in defeat. I told my mother not to worry. The Germans would be our liberators. And I hoped that I might see my father and brother again.

While I was standing in a field outside of the city I saw a distant soldier approaching, followed by others. He walked down a narrow track of road. As he got closer, I saw that his face was painted with daubs of olive and rust. Twigs and leaves were stuck in the netting that covered his helmet. His face was attenuated by strain and fatigue. When he walked up to me he pointed his weapon, and then he spoke to me in German with an accent I found hard to place. He asked me what place this was. His voice was hoarse. I told him that this was Tokmak and that there were many ethnic Germans here who would welcome him as a liberator. Not long after that the Germans arrived in force. *Panzerkampfwagen. Sturmgeschütz.* They rolled over the fields – armour mounted upon tracks and wheels tearing through the black earth, crushing, grind-ing, sharp blades swinging through tall, yielding grass. I watched as the force and the power of the German army rolled by us and I cheered and hoped it might crush the Communists who had stolen my father and brother.

Later, other soldiers came, special soldiers, and special police who occupied the old school near the centre of the town that the Soviet police had used for their headquarters. That was the last place that I'd seen my father. I'd watched him being taken through the front doors with a Soviet policeman holding one of his arms. Now I saw different men milling about the front of the building. Some wore black uniforms with ss runes on their collars and white skulls on the front of their forage caps. They made lists of all the men who were of military age, and each was ordered to report to the police headquarters for screening and interrogation.

I reported to this building the morning after I received my summons, which was served by a soldier, because my name was on a list. I was nervous, of course, because I did not know what it meant. There was much activity in the building at that time and I saw soldiers and police carrying boxes and furniture through the wide doors of the front entrance and up the flights of stairs. I was directed to a room on the second floor. I entered and saw that the room was almost empty except for a long table in the centre. At one end of the table sat three officers. I was ordered to remain standing in front of them. One of the officers did all the talking. He questioned me in German. He asked me how old I was. I told him that I was seventeen. He asked me if I spoke Russian. I said that I did. He told me he needed volunteers for a kommando and to act as interpreters. "Will you enlist?" he asked. One of the other men was writing something down. The third simply stared at me, through me.

I looked at these men. They wore gloves and shiny black boots. They had the bearing of conquerors, and revealed no lack of confidence but rather projected a look of profound arrogance. I thought of the Russian policemen who had arrested my father. I thought of the soldiers I had seen in retreat, my brother perhaps among them or left behind. I thought of the victorious German tanks that had rolled through the town and across the fields in pursuit. And I felt at that moment that I was adrift, hovering in a narrow space between two worlds. I wondered much later if I had a choice. I wondered if I could have refused. But it had not occurred to me to say no. I joined willingly and I felt then as if I had surrendered myself to a force that was beyond my control, or to fate, like a vessel caught in the throes of a relentless current: SS runes, a little white death's head.

Today, as I write, I try to remember the face of that officer, the one who did all the talking. He smiled when I said I would volunteer. He said I was a good German, and he told me that the German forces were here to protect us, to protect our towns and our farms and our colonies. It was good and proper for me to serve, he told me. He said it was my duty because there was still much fighting to be done and many difficult tasks to perform.

Eight of us from the Tokmak region joined that day, including two boys I knew from Halbstadt. We were all seventeen years old and had gone to school together before the war. The old men were permitted to remain behind. Everyone else of military age had been taken by the Communists in the months before the war.

II

I live in Winnipeg now. In this last week of October I can sense winter's approach. I watch from my kitchen window as leaves flutter down from the trees overhead and spread themselves across my yard in random patterns of red, yellow, and brown – the detritus of a summer season now vanished. I have lived in this house, this great old stone house, for thirty years. It was the home that my wife chose because of its beautiful garden, at the end of a street lined with great sheltering elms. She is gone now and the garden lies dormant, waiting for the snow to fall. And though the elms remain, they too are subject to the seasons, their branches soon to be stripped bare by the dry, blustery winds that will bring the ice and the cold.

This summer a family moved into the house next door. The man and the woman both seem quite youthful, and have a child, a little boy who always plays in the front yard. Today the man came to my door and offered to clear the leaves from my yard; he had a roundish, pleasant face atop a slightly stocky body that thickened somewhat in the middle. I guessed that he was in his mid-thirties. I thanked him for his offer and gladly accepted because the work would have been a strain. He told me his name was John and I told him my name was Fred. I never use the name Friedrich here.

He returned minutes later with a rake and some plastic bags, and he brought his young son along too. I heard the boy singing and laughing and chattering away while his father worked in the yard at the rear of my house. Wearing a pair of oversized rubber boots, the boy tramped about in the leaves that his father had heaped into piles near the garden I'd planted at the back of the yard. Years before, I had dug a shallow pit just to the right of the garden. Then I'd lined the pit with dark red bricks and sealed them with mortar. Now the man built a fire in the pit and I watched from a distance as the blinking flames formed darting shapes like long and sinewy fingers clutching and stretching, then curling about the leaves, squeezing them into ash. The man worked all morning raking and gathering the leaves while they continued to fall from the sky.

I prepared a lunch and when it was nearly noon I brought the food outdoors on a tray so they could eat on the stone terrace behind the house. The man ate hungrily and the boy munched and nibbled in a peripatetic fashion and then he went out to the garden to play some more. His father warned him to stay away from the pit. The air seemed motionless now that the flames had subsided. But the ash in the pit still smouldered, and thin trails of pale smoke flowed upwards in determined streams that intertwined and separated with easy fluidity.

After the man had eaten, we spoke about the weather and the winter that was to come. He warned me it would be one of the coldest yet. I did not ask him how he knew this, but he made this assertion with such confidence that I believed him nevertheless. I nodded as he spoke, and thought how he seemed so young to have a family and a business and a house. While we chatted, we kept our eyes on the boy, who sat in the garden playing with a set of plastic soldiers. Then a breeze whirled up, causing the trees to waver and shudder, and the air was filled again with a mass of falling leaves. The young boy looked up as they fell all around him. The man laughed, too, and said this type of work was never done. I thanked him again for his kindness. Then he walked away from the patio and back out to the yard and began the process of raking all over again.

The air was cool, and the acrid scent of the burning leaves filled my nostrils. I stared out at my garden, which had been full and fecund in summer. Now it was chopped down and trimmed: trimmed by morning frosts, hoary preludes to winter snows; trimmed by my own hands, by clippers and a spade; trimmed to a barren patch of soil dotted with ubiquitous leaves.

The young boy continued to play at war and I listened for a while as he tried to imitate the cracks and whistles of gunfire and grenades and the final cries of the violently slain. As the battle ensued, he moved some of his tiny troops across the surface of the garden, knocking the others down into the little holes and trenches he had made in the soil. I continued to watch but my mind began to drift. I smelled the burning leaves again and felt the chill in the air. I thought of a city named Mariupol and began to feel very tired.

In Tokmak I was sworn in and received a uniform. After one month of training in the use of firearms I was ordered to join a special kommando in Mariupol. I travelled there from Tokmak in a military transport truck stuffed with supplies for the kommando and driven by Richmaier. He was a good ten years older than I and well over six feet tall. His features were coarse and ruddy, his skin tanned and leathery. But his eyes were very bright and blue and I soon learned that he loved to talk. The two of us sat side by side in the cab and he spoke incessantly that whole day as we rumbled along the terrible smashed road that led to Mariupol and took me farther and farther from my home.

This had been a farming region, but it was now scarred by the recent battles that had been fought through here. I saw the burnt-out hulks of smashed tanks and army vehicles pushed off to the sides of the road. We passed the remnants of villages that had been destroyed and, in the distance, columns of black smoke rose on the horizon.

Richmaier told me that he had been a farmer in a German colony situated only ten kilometres from Tokmak. A few months before the war he was drafted into the Russian army, where he was trained as a truck driver. His unit dissolved and fled well in advance of the Germans, so he deserted and burned his uniform and tried to return to his home.

He said, "When I arrived there was nothing left. The colony had been obliterated. The farms were destroyed and everyone was gone – my wife, my parents, everyone, gone. The Russians had taken them or killed them, but left no trace. The Germans arrived the next day, and I told them

I could drive and speak Russian, so they let me enlist. What could I do? I had no place left to go. And I wanted to get even, too."

When we entered Mariupol, Richmaier pointed to a sign posted on a wall. I saw others like it posted farther down the street. "Look, do you see?" He pointed with one large finger thick as rope. "And there also," he said. "They've been posted throughout the city, so there can be no mistake. That's the best way to do it. That way they come to us and we don't have to round them up. It's much better this way: there's less panic, less confusion. They're reassured by it; it makes them think that no harm will come to them."

"Who are you talking about?" I asked.

"The Jews, of course. Here, look."

He stopped the vehicle beside one of the signs so I could read it.

The sign was really a poster made of thick yellow paper. It bore the signatures of the members of the Jewish council and the name of ss Commander Zeetzen:

In recent days there have been incidents of violence perpetrated against the Jewish population by non-Jews. These acts will continue as long as the Jewish population is distributed over the entire city area. To prevent any further such acts the German police organs see no alternative but to resettle the entire Jewish population in a special district outside of Mariupol.

Resettlement measures will be commenced on October 19, 1941. . . .

All Jews must bring their personal papers, the keys to their lodgings, and any money and valuables in their possession. One piece of luggage will be permitted per Jew.

They were commanded to gather at a location near the centre of the city at seven the next morning.

I was billeted with the other kommando men at a former barracks inside the city. The interpreters were all housed in one room. There were eight of us at that time, including Richmaier. He told me that the kommando was made up of another eighty Germans and a company of helpers that were called HiWis. "They are a mixed lot," he said, "Ukrainians, Russians, Cossacks, but they are usually quartered separately from the interpreters and the Germans."

I was very tired from the long journey, but I was unable to sleep. The events of the journey, the newness and the oddness of it all, had given me little time to reflect. It was only now, as I lay on a rough cot, eyes open and the others sleeping around me, that I realized that I might never see my family or my home again. I was now a part of something that was much bigger than I, and this filled me with a deep sadness.

The next morning at first light we paraded before Zeetzen. He addressed us in a square outside the barracks while the officers of his staff stood to the side. His voice was high and sharp and seemed to cut through the cold air. I was very nervous, and was unable to eat with the others before the parade. Now I felt light-headed and regretted not having tried to force down a morsel.

Zeetzen said that he welcomed the new additions to the kommando, so I knew that I was not the only one. Then he spoke of the operation before us: "Those of you who are newly attached to the kommando will have to pay careful attention to your comrades. They are experienced in carrying out these extraordinary actions. Observe them and learn from them. This morning the kommando will commence a major resettlement action and it is expected that this operation will take three days to complete. It is only natural that you will find the tasks at hand disagreeable; to feel otherwise would be inhuman. But your duty requires you to overcome such instincts. These are difficult times, but we must, all of us, adjust. Our duty can require nothing less. These things must remain unspoken."

A collection of transports was parked beside the barracks. We kommando men climbed into the back of the first two trucks in the column. These were Wehrmacht transports painted a chalky shade of grey, and the rear platform of each was covered and enclosed with a heavy tarpaulin stretched over several supporting poles. On the sides of the cab doors there was an insignia of the ten of hearts. The rest of the trucks remained empty. They would be used to relocate the Jews. Zeetzen and the officers rode in two cars.

We drove from the barracks to the centre of the city. There we waited. Some of the kommando got out of the trucks and stood about, talking and smoking. I stayed in the truck, sitting on the edge of the hard bench. I watched as the people began to arrive in twos and threes, then in larger groups – families, I supposed. Many were dressed in their nicest clothes, and I wondered if they were hoping to make a good impression. They clutched suitcases and other types of bags, one bag per person. They stood close to one another at the gathering place, and the group became larger as others arrived. A few, I could see, were warily looking over at the trucks and the kommando men. They whispered to some of the others, motioning and pointing, some looking distressed. But most of the people remained quite calm. They didn't stare at the line of empty trucks. They didn't stare at the group of men wearing grey and tan and black who hovered at one side of the square, their carbines over one shoulder, their high black boots grinding into the cobblestones. They might have thought that we were no longer here.

I saw men with beards and braided locks of hair talking to one another. Beside them the women also congregated, women of all ages. There was much talking and even the sounds of laughter. There were many children, too, who ran about playing, yelling, giggling, as if it were all some mysterious adventure. I saw the young, and the old, women, men, children, families. It was not unlike a kind of picnic, or perhaps a fair, like the ones my parents took me to in Molotschna or Tokmak when I was a boy.

Then another transport truck arrived, and a dozen or so HiWis descended and gathered into a group. Their uniforms were ill-fitting. Some wore grey like the interpreters, others wore brown. They were quiet and sullen-looking as they eyed the crowd that swelled within the confines of the square.

A row of tables was set up at one side of the square and the Jews were ordered to form lines in front of each table to report and produce their papers. This process took much longer than expected and it was not until almost noon that Baumer shouted the order to load the first groups into the transport trucks. Richmaier translated the order and the Ukrainians moved into the square, calmly motioning to the first line of Jews that it was time to leave. No one yelled, no one pushed or shoved; it was all quite orderly. I saw an old man with a carved white cane helped up a stepladder onto the back of the truck by one of the Ukrainians, who before had stood scowling on the perimeter. Now he smiled at the old man and gave him a pat as he climbed the ladder. A woman held her baby and then passed it to another woman as she climbed upwards. A young couple held each other's hands and climbed one after the other.

Before getting into the trucks, the Jews were told to leave their belongings in a special pile. Hearing this, an old woman pressed a tiny satchel to her chest and began to weep. A young woman close beside her, pretty with dark eyes and a yellow kerchief, her daughter perhaps, tried to take the satchel from her, but the old woman fell to her knees, keeping her arms tight against the bag as she began to wail. An interpreter named Penner ran over to this first group, and in a voice that was loud enough for all to hear but without anger, said, "Do not be distressed. Your baggage will travel in separate trucks but it will be delivered to you at the end of the journey."

This seemed to reassure the others in the group. I watched as the young woman with the yellow kerchief gently eased the satchel from the old woman. She spoke softly to her and kissed her head. Penner directed her to place the satchel beside the trucks, where a pile had been formed. She smiled at Penner as if to give thanks. He smiled back and then gestured towards the truck to tell her that she must now board. He even helped the old woman, who wept silently now as she was lifted into the back of the truck.

As the people disappeared into the transports, the piles of bags and sacks and bundles beside each truck grew higher. When the trucks were filled to capacity, the order was given by Baumer to move out. Richmaier and Penner got back into our truck, as did some of the other kommando men. There was a great rumbling as the column began to move. Our vehicle was to escort from the rear, so we waited for the others to pass. The tarpaulin flap at the back of each transport was folded out and tied open. I caught a glimpse of white faces peeking out from the darkness and noticed again the ten of hearts painted on the side of each door.

As there were still many Jews left in the square, some of our men remained as guards. We drove past the piles of bags and suitcases, and I saw that they were unattended. I asked one of the German kommando men beside me, "Who keeps track of the owners of all of those bags? How are they returned?"

He looked at me with a grin, then shook his head a little and looked away. I turned my head and looked at the other kommando men in the truck, but no one spoke and there was a kind of silence, a smell of diesel, and the throaty rumbling sounds of the engines of each truck. I stared back at the piles of baggage and watched how they grew smaller as we drove farther from the square. I felt quite lonely then, and closed my eyes for a while.

There were eight trucks in the column, including the kommando transports, and I estimated that this convoy travelled several kilometres until it was well outside the city. We arrived at an empty field near the edge of a ravine. We circled around the column, which had come to a halt, and then our truck stopped and we backed up so that the truck was perpendicular to the line of transports.

The silence was broken.

It started as a kind of roaring that began at the end of the column farthest from me where the first truck had halted, and as the noise worked its way along the line it gained strength, spilling over into violence and barely controlled rage. I saw the kommando transformed before my eyes as each man altered his countenance. There were no more reassuring voices and no more smiles or gentle gestures. Everything changed in those moments – as if light and life was replaced by a blankness or a void.

I saw Sergeant Baumer's face first. He had come around to the back of our truck and yelled at us to get out. He pointed at me because I was new and told me to stay by his side. So I jumped down and tried to follow him, but Richmaier and Penner got ahead of me. I saw that Baumer had run over to the last truck in the line. He banged the butt of his carbine several times against the lower side panel of the truck. I could see that some of the people were standing now, looking out of the trucks, alarmed by the yells and the sudden clatter. Richmaier caught up to Baumer and began yelling at the Jews to get out of the trucks.

I looked down the line of trucks. The kommando men had descended upon them like a horde of bees. I ran towards

Baumer, who now stood a few paces back from the last two
trucks in the column. Penner was at one truck and
Richmaier at the other. They kept yelling at the Jews, who
were struggling to dismount. There were no stepladders now,
no helping hands or gentle pats. In the panic the younger
ones tried to get by the old. At the truck right in front of me
a young boy, jostled from behind, lost his grip on the tarpaulin and tumbled to the ground. He struggled to get up. His
face, now bloodied, peered upwards with a look of stupefac-
tion and utter fear. The others watched from above, now
refusing to jump down from the truck.

Richmaier pointed at two of the Ukrainians standing by
and they hoisted themselves into the truck. The Jews moved
back behind the tarpaulin, but to no avail. The Ukrainians
began flinging people out of the truck, shoving them and
striking them with the barrels of their carbines. I saw the old
woman who had had the satchel tossed out with horrible
ease. The force of the fall seemed to crush her like a mallet
and she remained in a heap below the truck. The young
woman could be of no help to her now. The second
Ukrainian had held her back while the first dealt with the old
woman. When she struggled to get free he let go of her and
swung the butt of his rifle up into her face. The yellow kerchief was knocked away and she tumbled to the ground, like
the old woman before her. They lay motionless, side by side.
Once the truck was empty, the two HiWis jumped down.
They shouldered their carbines and dragged the unconscious
women by the arms and dumped them beside the long rows
of Jews that had now been formed to stand in a line running
parallel to the line of trucks.

All the way along the line and on both sides I saw that the kommando men had formed a cordon. They were all bellowing, gesturing, and shoving at some of the people until the line of Jews began to move forward. Baumer told me to follow him, and Richmaier and Penner caught up to us a few seconds later. Baumer ordered some of the Russian HiWis to remain by the trucks to act as guards and to ensure that no one stayed behind. Penner translated the order and we moved farther down the line. I was breathless now and could not think. I simply followed Baumer and Richmaier and we moved quickly beside that long, long line.

I could see that the work of the kommando was carried out in a very efficient manner, which I assumed was a result of an accumulation of previous actions like the one that now unfolded. Despite the apparent confusion, the yelling and the violence, there was a kind of order to it all, as if everyone knew which part to play.

I struggled to keep up with Baumer and the two other interpreters. We moved quickly to the head of the line, and I could see now that the Jews were being herded towards a path that led down into the opening of a ravine. Three or four hundred yards to the rear the trucks remained parked, but already two of them had begun to leave as this long pitiful column wound its way down.

Several dozen Jews were forced further down the path as the rest of the line was halted and several kommando men stood by. We passed this spot until I could see where the line, where all of this, was leading. Someone had dug a long, wide trench that deepened the ravine. The fresh sandy soil formed a parapet on either side of the trench. A few yards away the first group of Jews stood huddled together. Now there were no smiles, no children playing, no close discussions. They looked like ghosts to me, hollowed out by the terror of their present circumstances.

Penner ordered this group to strip off their clothes and throw them in a pile. He kept shouting, "Strip! Strip!" Some of the women began to wail, while others gasped and silently obeyed his command. They were so close to me, maybe six metres away, that I could feel the intensity of their fear. I felt choked by it. Panic welled up inside me and I began to tremble. I made to turn away, and I think I would have run at that moment, but Baumer was there and must have been watching me. He grabbed my shoulder and shoved me forward with enough force that I stumbled. He would not let me turn away.

"If you run I'll shoot you myself. You'll see worse things than this, I promise you that. After a month of this shitty business you'll be an old hand and you'll cease to care." He wasn't yelling; his voice was quite calm, quite rational. I could no longer move.

I saw Penner, the interpreter, look over at Baumer, anticipating the order.

"Take them in groups of ten," Baumer said to Penner.

Penner obeyed and moved in amongst the group and pointed at ten of the huddled forms. They were all young women. Some of them wept, others seemed to be praying, and others remained mute, staring forward with fixed, wide eyes that seemed to bulge with fear. A line of seven kommando men stood a short distance away opposite the trench. I recognized two of the Russians HiWis, Psarev and Skripkin, the red-headed driver, Brunschen. The rest were ss, all Germans. They were the older hands in the kommando.

Penner had his pistol out and waved it at the women, gesturing, yelling at them as they hurried past and up onto the dirt parapet. The women stood for a moment on the mound of soil above the deep, wide trench, breathless, their mouths gaping, drawing in air in short gasps. I saw how they tried to cover themselves by placing their hands over their breasts or between their legs. Some seemed barely able to stand. They stood there as if suspended for a moment, above that earth. Then a volley from the firing party tore into the women, through them, and they seemed to disintegrate as the force of the bullets hurled them off the parapet and backwards into the ditch below.

Soon another group of ten, all men this time, was herded forward in single file up onto the parapet. One of the men had soiled himself and a watery, brown effluence ran down the inside of his legs. Psarev made a joke, but the laughter of the others was drowned out by the volley of carbines and machine guns. They were shot down like the women that preceded them: heads snapping back, limbs pale and flopping, as they careered over the side into the blackness of the trench.

I had no sense of time as I watched row after row appear on that parapet and then disappear.

I took my turn on the firing line when the others needed to be relieved. But I have no memory now of how I held my carbine and whether my hands shook or how I must have reloaded my weapon after firing it so many times. I fired as if in a dream and I don't remember if I ever pulled the trigger, but I know that I must have. We all had to shoot, at least once. I saw the young woman on the parapet, the one with the yellow kerchief. The kerchief was gone now; in its place was a wide, long gash that gleamed black and red. The wound had swollen her eyes shut, so another woman was holding her arm, and she guided her up to the edge of the trench, and I noticed that she continued to hold her until a volley tore them apart and away.

In my mind's eye I can still see Baumer, grey-faced and sweating, ordering the men to fire. And I can see Skripkin, the Russian, walking up and down the edge of the parapet with his pistol drawn, pausing from time to time to fire down into the piles of bodies to finish off any survivors. Sometimes little spouts of blood and pulp splashed upwards and onto his black boots.

At dusk we paused.

At the end of this first day I stood alone watching Skripkin as the other kommando men headed back up to the trucks. Then Baumer was beside me and he said that this was called an *Aktion*, and he told me to go with the others back to the trucks. As I obeyed I heard him say, as if reassuringly, that it would not be so bad for me the next time.

The second day was just as bad. At dawn we returned to that ravine. A thick frost coated the ground and the bodies we'd left piled up in the ditch. The dark red stains had seeped through the white, and the air smelled of blood. I remember Skripkin standing at the parapet all that second day firing his pistol again and again and again until there were no more bullets, and all the time the leaves fell from the trees until they were finally bare.

On the third day, as the sun set, we left that place and

made our way back to Mariupol and the army barracks. I rode in the first truck of the column and the other kommando trucks followed. I felt that my lungs were full of dust; the smell of cordite, sharp and burning, had seeped into my tunic and filled my nostrils. There was a darker smell too, rank, sweet, and metallic. That smell seemed to grow stronger now; every man in that truck, in the kommando, reeked of it now. The stench of it sunk into the recesses of each pore and beyond into the deep fabric of our being until I could see an image of it in my mind.

Horror. A silent horror. Hushed, as if the sound of it were frozen.

In the truck, not a man spoke. None of us could speak. We sat hunched over, dark in the fading light, each of us rocking back and forth with the movement of the transports. I felt a presence, a dizziness, like a blackness enfolding me, and like a hand it took me in its grasp. I felt it squeeze the warmth out of my body and a coldness rush in to fill that void. Then a thousand black dots seemed to explode into my eyes and I was whisked away.

I awoke, perhaps seconds later. In my faint I had spilled forward into the centre of the truck. Richmaier helped me up; then Maar, another interpreter, poured some water from his canteen across my lips. But they said nothing to me. No one spoke. I pulled out a handkerchief and wiped the bitter vomit from my chin and cheek. I held my sides and stomach and wrapped them with my arms and hands and held on to myself as I leaned back into the darkness of the truck. I tried to think of my home and of my mother but I could see nothing but the blackness seeming to form around me.

I

I walked to work today, as I always do, watching lanes of cars whip past me at high speeds, honking, screeching, roaring as if every driver in Ottawa were fuelled by the chips on their shoulders and a death wish. I turned from O'Connor onto Laurier in time to see a row of transit buses arrive from the great suburban outland. As I walked towards them, I entered a kind of melee as the smell of diesel enveloped me and hordes of commuters spilled out of the doors of each bus. They'd travelled for miles, many from pre-fab neighbour-hoods of tedious conformity with names like Langley Estates and Cotswold Manors, carved and stencilled out of swamps and fields and forests.

I recalled a line from a poem. "I had not thought death had undone so many."

As I ducked and dodged my way through the crowd I was

pushed aside by some, so eager were they to be prompt. One man, with a nasty little moustache and rat-like eyes, swung his umbrella in front of him like a rapier, saying with a screechy small voice, "Excuse me, excuse me," so as to part the crowds and allow him passage. I saw many men with raincoats and umbrellas, smugly clutching briefcases and valises that seemed to boast, *we're stuffed with papers and documents of national import.* They were as likely to be filled with rubbish, pilfered pens and office supplies, and yellowy plastic lunch containers with leaky freshness seals.

There were women amongst them, sporting sensible short bobs, with tedious straight bangs and large round glasses. They wore knee-length skirts, which hovered above thick calves, and matching blazers of reckless shades of beige or blue. I watched them trot past me, some wearing pink and white sneakers, carrying shoe bags and briefcases, no doubt concealing the same type of rubbish with a feminine slant.

The activity on the street intensified as people dashed to and fro. Just as they'd spilled out of buses and cars I now saw them spill into ugly white buildings with black reflecting windows, some of the diehards pausing to suck on a butt, while others filtered in through glass doors. The old, the young, the fast, the slow, the eager, the slothful were all there in a rainbow coalition of commuters. The rite would be repeated in reverse this afternoon at precisely four-thirty.

I could see the man with the rapier umbrella well in front of me now, still clearing a path before him. I ducked to the left and spun through a revolving door, but no one followed.

The great horde continued to flow by on the sidewalk, and I walked across the quiet lobby and through the open elevator doors to ascend as far as the sixth floor.

I examined the early morning through a plate-glass window the full height and width of my tiny, cluttered office. Outside, the sky was a dense mass of cloud, a nebulous haze clinging to the lower rooftops and smothering the higher towers of the cityscape. Somewhere overhead, above that grey mire, tiers of jet planes hovered and circled, meandering without resolve and awaiting instructions. This was the present, but I dealt only with the past.

October 16, 1994. Today was my birthday. I had turned thirty-three: a soon to be unemployed thirty-three-year-old historian with few prospects on the horizon.

My office was located eight blocks from my apartment on the sixth floor of an aging, dreary building at the centre of a dreary block on a dreary corner of Bank and Queen. It was a building that, in a city otherwise grey in character, texture, and spirit – the very embodiment of grey – possessed the relative distinction of being painted beige. The exterior was made of brick and concrete corroded and stained by the efficacious scouring of harsh winters and humid summers. Conforming to the structure's exterior, the interior walls of the sixth floor were painted beige as well, and had remained so for at least two decades; the only notable exception to this surfeit of beige was the wall-to-wall mauve carpet, simultaneously offsetting and offputting.

For six years the sixth floor had been home to the Special Prosecutions Unit, described at its inauguration by the

then–Directing Minister of Foreign Matters as an "organiza-
tion dedicated to the swift investigation and prosecution of
Nazi war criminals residing in Canada." In the curious world
of the civil service, a contradictory world made up of long
highways with only slow lanes, the use of acronyms was
commonplace, revealing a deepset reluctance to use complete
words or names. And so the words "Special Prosecutions
Unit" would and did eventually disappear from the government lexicon, to be replaced by a new locution where the
first letter of each word would suffice, spelled out in this
manner: SPU.

I have worked in this office for all of those six years, one
of the first historians hired along with a team of other historians, lawyers, researchers, translators, and police investigators
that, up until a few months ago, numbered, all told, about
forty. In the course of those years I have churned out a veritable life's work of words: memos and letters that confirmed
other memos and letters, historical reports that backed up
and enhanced other historical reports, and more reports after
that, continuing assessments, backgrounds and projections,
regurgitations and classifications and reclassifications.
Everything was stored away, not only in the memory banks
of my computer, but also within the confines of a long,
narrow storage room that safely housed a legion of brown
manila files.

I stepped back from the window and sat down in my
swivel chair. Then I leaned towards my computer and pushed
the round white button that every morning brought that
plump, beige box to life. It made a thin winding-up sound

followed by a series of jerking, mechanical cyber-grunts. The screen lit up and evolved from black to glowing green. A small white box popped up in centre of the screen and invited me to enter my private password. *Fuck you*, I typed, and then I pressed the "enter" key. The little box vanished, quickly replaced by another that extended a cheery greeting: *Good morning D. Connor*, confirming that I still existed. In a second the greeting also vanished and was replaced by a new layout on the screen, filled with a cluster of tiny icons, like a miniature marquee that boasted of coming events.

I left my office and walked down the hall to the coffee room. Someone had made a fresh pot and I filled my cup almost to the brim, leaving a tiny gap for a splash of milk. When I opened the refrigerator I discovered that there was not a drop of milk to be had, so I cursed the world again and resorted to flinging two sloppy teaspoons of powdered whitener into my cup. The stuff floated in a lump in the centre of the cup until it collapsed and crumbled to a muck that spread across the surface of the coffee, like scum on a slough. I broke it up further with a few hasty stirrings with a much-used spoon that I'd found abandoned in a drawer.

Boot up the computer. Get a cup of coffee. The ritual of my everymorning was complete. Things would change as things were wont to do, and always, it seemed, when change was most inconvenient and most undesired. These mornings, I knew, were to be short-lived, and my days in this place decidedly numbered. But that was old news. I'd known for two months now that the SPU would be closing down.

The news, like most disagreeable news having a nearly universal application to a particular place, didn't come from an identifiable human voice. Rather, the message was delivered in a government memo, addressed to everyone concerned and not *from* any one person in particular.

It was dated June 14, 1994, and it read as follows:

Due to current fiscal restraints and a limitation on resources the Special Prosecutions Unit (SPU) will shortly commence a program of conclusive downsizing which will include an 85% reduction of current staff levels within three months and a total sunsetting reduction to be effected within six months.

Even to an initiate like myself, accustomed to the clumsy euphemisms so prevalent in the civil service, the message was not at first abundantly clear. I had to read this through a couple of times to appreciate the gist of it. To an outsider it did require some translation. In short, it said that someone had decided to turn off the money tap and divert the funds to some other initiative, plan, or grand scheme, and that meant you and you and I and, yes, you too, would shortly be at loose ends. There you had it.

The suddenness of it all did come to me as a shock, but in retrospect I should not have been surprised. I should have recognized that the place was doomed to unravel. But as if constrained by a determined kind of myopia, I never really looked beyond the lines in my historical reports that hovered before my eyes in the green glow of my computer monitor, like skywritings suspended in the ether.

The lawyers were the first to flee. Trained in a profession premised upon self-interest and relativism disguised as healthy ambition and pragmatism, this should have been expected. I could not really blame them, though. I'd have done the same had I a place to go. Some were experienced prosecutors before their stint at the SPU, so they were whisked off to other prosecution units without much ado. For the others there was always some superfluous government agency or regulatory branch in need of a warm body with a law degree.

Digby Hunt, the most devoted of the lawyers, was the last of them to leave, albeit under a bit of a cloud. There had been some "irregularities" and "an incident." It made little difference, since for weeks beforehand he'd known that some kind of axe was about to fall (or, in his case, a number of little axes that did the same trick). After the June announcement he had become increasingly despondent, moping about the sixth floor, gloomily contemplating the increasing number of vacant offices. No more investigations, no more trips overseas, no more elongated witness-interview trips to the exotic climes of western Ukraine.

When the little axes did fall upon Digby's luckless head, like so many pieces of shrapnel, they stung him but they weren't fatal. Digby could not, of course, be fired since he was a permanent government employee – doubtless even acts of treason, piracy, or intimidating Parliament wouldn't warrant such a drastic sanction. Instead he was whisked off with the speed of a wish to the crepuscular chambers of the Department of Research, Education, and Knowledge (DREK) to act as in-house counsel. It was not readily apparent that

DREK actually *required* the services of a solicitor, but since every other self-respecting government agency had at least one, the deep thinkers at DREK felt the omission had to be remedied. They weren't fussy, mind; Digby would do just fine. He was sent to a place where he did not wish to go, where he was neither needed nor really wanted, except for show.

He came to visit me a few weeks after he started at DREK. He claimed that he still had some odds and ends to pick up, but I suspected that this was a pretence. I think he wanted one last look at the place he had practically called home. He slumped down in a chair opposite my desk. I was happy to see him and extended my hand. He shook it without a trace of vigour and I noticed that his hand seemed unnaturally soft and clammy, like wet putty. He looked thoroughly depressed and a little shellshocked, as if he'd taken too many of those allergy tablets with dire warnings on their labels about chainsaws and heavy machinery. He seemed to have gained weight also: he looked thicker around the middle and I thought I saw a tiny pillow of flab forming beneath his chin. I felt my own waistband for a moment, just to reassure myself.

Digby was over six feet, with a large frame that veered towards the portly from time to time if he didn't take care. It was rather like the Watch on the Rhine. When the flab re-emerged, he'd revert to a Spartan diet and fling himself into an exercise regimen, so that the pesky flab was pincered and trimmed, though destined to return. Flab loved Digby, it craved him, it had a giggling crush on him. It always wanted to hang around him. It liked the fleshy spot under his chin, the comfy sacks just above his hips, and the welcoming folds of his belly. But Digby was determined to prevail and never lacked tenacity. He battled the unrequited love of that adoring flab with a vengeance, in the only way he knew how: he'd beat it back with his squash racquet, starve it into submission with fruits and fibre, or try to run it into the ground with brand-new trainers and nylon shorts. But the flab never took it personally and always came back for more.

The agitating powers of stress and depression allow for certain consolations to a chosen few. In some, prevailing melancholia effected the *loss* of weight and the cultivation of an oddly attractive haunted look, but Digby's constitution would not permit such a silver lining. When riddled with sadness, Digby's body convinced itself that the best bet was to store fat. He might just as well have spent the last few weeks at home washing down hearty portions of Stilton, fried chicken, and sausage with tumblers of milkshakes and port wine.

"It could be worse," he said, in a way that suggested that he felt it could not possibly *be* worse. "I can see Hull from my window."

I thought of something I might say, some platitude, some truism, something trite and folksy, but nothing sprang to mind. I sighed and looked down at my shoes, which I noticed were brown and ugly with frayed laces. I forgot about Digby for a moment and thought that I really ought to buy a new pair of shoes. Something sporty perhaps.

My mind returned to the subject of Digby as he began to speak. His voice was softer now, a pleasant voice, with a slight rasp. He started picking at a tiny stain on the knee of his pants.

"There's a big magnet in my building, on the floor below

me. It's part of some sort of research project." His voice suggested that this was a cause neither for optimism nor distress.

"What's it for?" I asked him, offering a mild tone of interest.

"What, the research facility?"

"No, the magnet. What is the magnet for?"

"I don't know, it's just some kind of oversized magnet positioned in a large room on the second floor right below my office and my arsehole. The damn thing's probably sending microwaves into my prostate. Of course no one will tell me why it's there in the first place, but then no one there talks to me anyway."

He kept picking at the stain. It looked like ketchup, or perhaps gravy.

"What kind of work do they have you doing?"

"*Work?* I don't work on anything. My telephone never rings, I never receive so much as a memo or a letter. Thank God they gave me a computer. I sit around all day and play games on the computer – Solitaire, Mine-sweeper, and Tank Commander – plus there's a trivia game called You Don't Know Dick. I've stared at that damn glowing screen so much this week I can't wear my contact lenses any more. Anyway, fuck it. How's things with you?"

I pointed to a pile of files in front of me on my desk. "I'm burying the bodies, Digby, you know that."

"I guess it's really over this time. No rumours of bailouts or last-minute funding to save the day?"

"What do you think?" I gave him a baleful look, and he shrugged and stared at the files. They were his old friends, files he'd nurtured and coddled, and helped through good times and bad. There were more files on my bookshelves, too. Piles of them. All dead files. Digby's orphans.

I planted my elbows on my desk and rested my chin in my hands for a moment and watched him sink into a brief reverie. Then he stood up as if he'd been yanked out of his seat.

"Oh, God! I have to go. I have an appointment with my lawyer."

My glance was a silent question mark.

"Bryndyce" he said. "She's going through with the divorce. It never rains, it pours."

"Shit," I said. "No chance you may get back together?"

"Not bloody likely. She's not exactly the forgiving type." He looked around the office another time and then looked back at me. "Good luck to you, Dennis. Maybe we'll go for a beer sometime."

"Yeah, that would be nice." Neither of us sounded like such an event was ever likely to occur. He gave me a wave and was gone.

Digby and I were never really friends and we never would be. It wasn't a question of likes or dislikes. I didn't hate him, though we had clashed from time to time when things began to go wrong and the office began to reek of frustration and despair. I never felt that there was a connection between us, but I think he tried to construct one. As things got worse for him he'd often come and sit in my office and tell me about his troubles with Bryndyce. I always tried to listen, or at least pretended to listen. I think by then he was simply fresh out of friends.

I'd met Bryndyce on a few occasions. They hosted a couple of office parties at their house two years before. She was pretty, with a small chin and round eyes, but I thought she had kind of a mean look to her, as if always waiting for an opportunity to ambush you. They'd met in 1988 in Toronto, where she'd been attending the Foreign Students Institute learning English. They married a year later. Digby told me that he'd first fallen in love with her because she had a Swiss-German accent and because she had curly hair. (It later revealed itself as a perm). She was born and raised in Switzerland, though her father was an American.

When I first met her she said to me, "My father may be American and my husband a Canadian, but my sensibilities will always remain devoutly European." I took that to mean she was odious in a well-rounded, cosmopolitan way.

The police investigators departed almost as swiftly as the prosecutors. All of them had arrived at the shores of the SPU by virtue of extended transfers from other police departments, and with these temporary positions decidedly now at an end, they were free to return to more conventional types of investigations. My favourite of that bunch was a Mountie named Gord Viaux. He was a giant of a man, and as a narcotics officer he'd specialized in portraying bikers and the like. He'd framed a photo of himself from those days, which he hung in his office at the SPU. It was a mug-shot, actually, taken after his arrest by a couple of Toronto detectives who thought they'd just cracked a cigarette-smuggling ring. He spent a night in jail but he gave one of the detectives some numbers to call. The telephone calls revealed that the cigarettes were not in fact stolen, and the big shit with the beard, tattoos, and stringy long hair was a cop playing a convincing part. There were no hard feelings and the detectives later sent him a blown-up version of the mug-shot, now displayed proudly in his office. Viaux would now be going back to his old narcotics unit. He took it all with a shrug. Worse things have happened, he told me.

His last day at the SPU I watched him plunk a cardboard file box on his desk. It made a clattering sound, since it was filled with a treasure trove of pens, paper, and yellow and pink highlighters. He took the framed mug-shot down from the wall and placed it on top of the purloined supplies. The other cops were now either gone or taking holidays to soak up the last muggy days of a hot August. Their office was a separate and cramped alcove off the main hallway of the sixth floor. It lacked a window, and the fluorescent lights flickered and hummed incessantly. There was a cupboard-sized coffee room which smelled faintly like stale milk. It contained a sink, a microwave, and a tiny refrigerator, each of which were uniformly dirty. The cops were unanimous: it was the nicest and biggest office space any of them had ever occupied.

"It'll take me a while to adjust," Viaux said, giving me a wink. "Now the bad guys I chase won't be in wheelchairs or walkers."

"They'll also still have a pulse." I said. Viaux chuckled. He rooted through the drawers of his desk to be sure he'd left nothing behind and pulled out an unopened box of ballpoint pens. "What the hell," he said. "In for a penny, in for a pound." He chucked it in the box with the rest of the stuff. This was to be his war chest for when he returned to the drug section. The SPU wasn't the only office with a cash-flow problem.

"No money for overtime, no money for long-term investigations. Christ! I'll probably have to buy my own bullets," he said.

When I laughed he extended one mighty paw in my direction. My hand disappeared into his, as if it had been swallowed by a baseball mitt. I wished him all the best.

Viaux had not been very happy during his service with the SPU. He had joined the unit at the ground floor, as I had, along with a handful of other police officers and several experienced criminal prosecutors. They had all been attracted by hiring bulletins that contained alluring promises of overseas travel and high-profile prosecutions of the modern world's worst villains. But Viaux came from a working environment where success was measured by the number of arrests and convictions and the length of a jail sentence. As he once said, we were playing catch-up with a war that had ended more than forty years before, and we were going to lose if we didn't move fast. Time was against us. Memories lapsed or vanished altogether and witnesses died with the inconvenient but predictable regularity of old age. I admired Viaux for seeing it through to the end when the other cops were voting with their feet, the allure of being a Nazi hunter having lost its cachet.

Although the SPU was launched with much fanfare and fresh-faced enthusiasm, no one thought the job would be an easy one. But within three years of its inception, the unit was successful in bringing its first case to trial. The accused was a Hungarian policeman in the war named Horvat, now a Canadian citizen living in Ottawa, and he had been complicit in the forcible deportation of Slovakian Jews to the charnel house of Auschwitz. I observed the whole of the proceedings, and the weaknesses of the case became readily apparent as the trial unfolded. The prosecutors, Goreman and Digby, had hoped to convict Horvat on the strength of an eyewitness and a series of deportation orders bearing Horvat's signature that would serve to corroborate the witness. The eyewitness's name was Jan Singer. He was called to the stand at the outset of the trial.

In 1944 Singer was a young man who served as one of Horvat's clerks, processing the onerous paperwork generated by the planned deportations. Singer remained in Horvat's service even while all the other Jews were being deported. He came to work each morning in an old coat with a yellow star sewn on it, until the day came when it was his turn to board the trains, the fact of his being a Jew outweighing his further usefulness as a clerk.

Aged beyond his years and traumatized by the camps, Singer's memory betrayed him at the very moment for which he had waited half a lifetime. In his mind's eye he lost sight of Horvat, whose name and face must have become confused with the images of a legion of blurred and distorted faces and names he knew, yet could somehow no longer pronounce out loud. When asked to identify Horvat in court, Singer could not. When asked to identify the signature on the orders, proof of Horvat's knowledge and guilt, the very papers that the young, frightened Singer had once carried with a trembling hand, he could not. And so in the hushed courtroom he began to weep, uncontrollably, hopelessly, unable to conquer that horror and unable to erase the one face, the one name, that emerged from the chaos that paralyzed his mind. *That* one face was clear.

"I remember one man clearly," he stated through sobs that made his voice sound like a child's, high-pitched and frail. "It was Mengele. As we got off the train he was the first man I saw. I swear to you today, his is the only face that I can remember now." Then he whispered, "It was always Mengele." He looked over at the jury when he said this. As he spoke he seemed to wither and age before the eyes of everyone in that courtroom.

"I can remember no one else now," he said, shaking his head. Then he was silent for a moment and looked down to the floor.

"Mengele robbed me of my memories.... *He* has robbed me of my soul."

That was all he could say. There were many more questions, but he could add little else. When finally there were no more questions to be asked and he was done, he stepped down from the witness stand, assisted by a clerk wearing a black robe, and then walked the length of the courtroom alone. As he passed by my seat near the back he seemed somehow transformed, as if reduced to the formlessness of a shadow or a ghost, passing silently across the cold marble floor.

The case took a turn for the worse after that. Horvat was by no means spry. His health had been questionable from the outset. He had been diagnosed with emphysema, diabetes (necessitating the amputation of a leg), and a variety of lesser but nonetheless nasty ailments. But it was his mental health that seemed most affected as the trial continued over days that turned to weeks. It came to a head when the police were called to Horvat's retirement complex late one night. Horvat, distressed, angry, wide-eyed, was stark naked, banging on the doors of his neighbours demanding that they return his shoes.

The police had to use force to arrest him, since he insisted he had a bus to catch for Kosice.

What followed was a lengthy motion in the absence of the jury to assess Horvat's competence to stand trial. Horvat had calmed down by then, indeed was now so calm as to be barely lucid and so he remained – one-legged and slumped in a corner of the courtroom, his bowels free to do as they pleased, his grip on life frail and tenuous – as he slipped off into a coma. The lawyers and the judge, absorbed in the excruciating legal minutiae that see substance subsumed by procedure, were oblivious to Horvat's burgeoning odour and took no notice of him until the court broke at noon. Attempts to revive him failed, he was rushed off to hospital, and on November 10, 1992, almost two years to the day after the charges were laid, proceedings against Horvat were adjourned *sine die*.

Horvat dispelled any hopes of a miraculous recovery by dying two months later.

It was no one's fault he was that old. It was no one's fault that the case was derailed. And yet it was lost on no one – not the police, not the lawyers, not even me – that there was a problem here that wasn't going away. Collectively there had been a lot of optimism that Horvat would be convicted. Now there were comments and criticisms from without (pundits and columnists with bones to pick and deadlines, politicians of the Official Opposition, malcontents of every strain) and within (grumblings behind closed doors and stage whispers in the hall). There was no consensus, outside or in: some were convinced the SPU had botched the case by waiting too long, others said the case was rushed and full of holes and that the unit had acted too hastily. You can never make everyone happy. They all have their own agendas.

A dull thud was felt in the office, followed by inertia, and thereafter a kind of rankness set in, the first essence of despair, like an ooze that crept down the dim halls and seeped through the decrepit carpet, through thin office walls, and spread through the storage rooms and the file rooms, finally settling, for a while, in the hard drives of every computer, like a virus born of malaise. I felt it grow stronger, by impercep- tible degrees. I saw it in others and I felt the first pangs of frustration as the process seemed to be grinding to a halt. The heady salad days of the SPU were coming to an end. Torn between fear of moving too fast and moving too slow, we simply couldn't get going again.

Staff lawyers came and went with alarming frequency, disillusioned or impatient, but they were always replaced by some new and eager face who'd greet me in the hallway.

"Hello," they'd say cheerily, "I'm new here." *No kidding.* Then they'd chatter away about how exciting it was all going to be when we got back into the courtroom. Of course eventually they'd be gone too, replaced by another, and another. The cops, like Viaux, tended to stick around longer. "All things considered, Dennis, it's a pretty good gig. The hours are good, the trips are bearable, and the meal allowance is not too bad. I'm not going to sweat it. I'll stick it out to the end."

Out of a fear of acting too rashly, the investigations were prolonged without an end in sight, and the files became engorged with increasing layers of paper – records, documents, reports, and memos – that transformed the SPU into an archive in its own right, while the search for living eyewitnesses carried on with diminishing rates of success. In the end, there were plenty of open files but no criminal charges in sight, and thus the SPU eventually came to an ignominious end.

The historians and research assistants scrambled about, lacking the protection of the permanent status afforded the lawyers and the cops, and well aware of the paucity of jobs within the civil service. The alternative was to limp back to one university or another in the hope that an associate professorship or a teaching assistant's position might be had.

Now I am left over from the great diaspora. I'm part of the skeleton crew, like that last helicopter leaving Saigon. There are five of us who remain, and our only task is to close the files so they'll be nicely wrapped and sealed and housed in a basement somewhere out of sight and out of mind. I suppose this is called file management or protocol; it's all one and the same. I received my instructions in memo form, one memo per file, which meant that I received about one hundred copies with virtually the same message; only the names were changed.

I began in no particular order. I simply piled them up in my office where I had room. My plan was to proceed pile by pile until the end. The last file was the exception. I had already selected it in advance, and its multiple volumes held a special place in the clattery twin drawers of my black credenza. The twin doors were shut but that file would remain open. I had no intention of closing it until the very last.

The memorandum for that file was still on my desk. It was dated September 15, 1994.

MEMORANDUM

TO: Dennis Connor, Staff Historian
FROM: Graham Goreman, Acting Director, Special Prosecutions Unit (SPU)
RE: Friedrich Reile, File #89-445;
As per the termination directive please prepare a file closure report for the above-noted suspect.

It always begins and ends with a report. After that there's never supposed to be anything left to be said. I would end with Reile. Before him I had one hundred and ten files to close down. That meant one hundred and ten reports to write, one hundred and ten ways of saying that the file must now be made to disappear. I estimated that it would take me roughly two months to finish the job, but I didn't much care about deadlines and neither did Goreman or anyone else. Goreman said that we could take as much time as we required. Whatever it took, he just wanted it all to go away quietly. I had no plans to finish the job early – I had nowhere else to go.

Goreman had been the lead prosecutor on the Horvat case, but had not assumed the role of *acting* director until December 1992. Goreman had replaced Doug Johst. I was sad to see Johst go. He was a gangly, avuncular fellow with a face that resembled the Cowardly Lion, but with no such lack of courage. He'd been a criminal prosecutor for twenty years and he brought to the SPU a keenness and an optimism that was infectious, and a love of extracurricular sports. My first day at work he had me in his office to welcome me aboard. He was like a kid, excited about the work and full of enthusiasm. Four years later he seemed quite tired and had lost some of his fire. He took a lot of the heat over the failure of the Horvat case.

He might have been able to ride it through, but he made a fundamental error of judgement, though it seemed for a while to be a wise move. He held an office meeting in the library boardroom on a Friday afternoon shortly after the trial's collapse. Attendance was mandatory. There were forty of us, all told, jammed into the narrow space located at one of the corners of the sixth floor. There weren't enough chairs, so most of us leaned up against the stacks that were filled with texts and law reports and statutes of all sorts. He started out strong. He told us that he would not countenance blame being foisted upon the police or his lawyers or his historians, not from within, not from without. He said he'd had a lengthy meeting with the management sector of the

Directorate of Foreign Matters that morning. He told them, as he was telling us now, that as director of the SPU he assumed all responsibility for any failure of this unit.

"That's the way it's supposed to be." And with a wry smirk he said, "That's why I'm paid the big salary. You look after the work and I'll deal with the people upstairs and all the naysayers and the chattering classes out there that want to dump all over my people. They don't understand that just because the case is a tough one to prosecute doesn't mean it won't be won, but it won't be won overnight."

It was his "Backs-to-the-wall" speech and it worked. I'd never heard anyone talk like that, and it cheered me up immensely. I think it made everyone in that cramped library want to jump right back into the fray. Even better, he'd organized a basketball game at the YMCA after work, lawyers versus historians, with the cops shared between the two teams, and beer afterwards at his house. There was nothing like sweat and liquor to make things well again.

Johst's efforts and integrity did not go unnoticed or unrewarded, and by Monday the following week he'd been summarily "re-deployed." That meant he was gone, gone with pay, but nonetheless gone.

"It was typical," Viaux said when he heard the news. "The only people this place will move quickly against are its own." He spat out those words like an old salt who'd seen it happen many times before.

Goreman, although in attendance, had remained mute throughout Johst's address. He exhibited little surprise on the Monday when the news quickly spread of Johst's departure. I noticed that he hid away for the rest of the day behind the closed door of his office, though he wasted little time moving from his previous working space to Johst's corner. Within a week, a couple of burly fellows in overalls had carefully boxed up all his office possessions for the arduous journey twenty yards farther down the hall. Discovering that the dimensions of his new digs were too small for his needs he had one of the walls moved over a few inches to make room for his leather couch and matching chairs.

Goreman was well-spoken and intelligent, but he betrayed a kind of uncertainty in his manner, as if less than assured of his connection to any time or place. He had none of Johst's verve or feistiness, though he'd been a lawyer for twenty years with the Criminal Prosecution Service in Vancouver before he walked through the SPU's swinging door. His arrival caused a bit of a stir. At the time of his appointment he had the singular distinction of having handled some of the Vancouver office's largest cases and, sadly for that office, its more significant defeats, all gleefully reported by the local media. It was never his fault, of course. It was always due to the mistakes of others, the failings and inadequacies of his co-counsel, the shortsightedness of his superiors, the incompetence of the police, weak judges, bad luck, bad weather, rancid karma. . . .

When Horvat was about to be indicted, the Directorate of Foreign Matters sent out a message nationwide that they were looking for a prosecutor. Goreman was the man they chose. It was rumoured that this appointment came partly as a result of some very enthusiastic lobbying by the senior prosecution staff in Vancouver. The fact that the trial would be held not in Vancouver but somewhere over the Rockies and far to the east – thus requiring Goreman's relocation for the duration of the trial – was a forfeiture to which that office was willing to accede. After the trial was done, Goreman never left. Maybe he simply wouldn't leave, or maybe no one wanted him back.

He was always well dressed, with silk ties, and cufflinks bearing his initials, G.A.G. They were fastened to the cuffs that poked out from beneath the arms of his dark-blue tailored suit. He made the rest of us look like bums, though that wasn't hard to do, since a large part of his competition was made up of cops and history grads. I guessed he was about fifty. He had a full head of wavy light-brown hair that was streaked with a glimpse of grey. He had thin, colourless lips and a complexion like wax, with a face so pale that one might question if his heart did beat and his blood flow. He was just shy of five-foot-eight and slim from his toes to his neck. His ears, pressed flat against his large head, were arched, forming a point at the top. His head seemed oddly out of proportion to the rest of his body, so that he looked rather like a well-tailored, carefully coiffed, deathly pale hobgoblin of a man who inhabited a very large office in a rather shaky kingdom.

I think of him now as a man without a country, or at least without a city-state, far from home, like the last governor of a moribund colony in some godforsaken corner of the world.

I recall him addressing the staff only once. It was a bitter, slushy Ottawa morning in January 1993. His timing was impeccable, as he had picked the first day back to work after the Christmas holidays to disabuse his people of any notion that the view on the horizon was an optimistic one.

He spoke with a vaguely British accent delivered in a thin, nasal voice. I learned later from Digby that Goreman had been born in Chilliwack, British Columbia, and didn't acquire the accent until a year of undergrad spent in Cambridge.

Goreman did not speak for long.

"Government Finance Committee has made it quite clear that the SPU budget may not be renewed beyond the end of the next fiscal year. In effect, we are now on probation. A year from now we could all be packing our bags."

"Now give us the bad news." someone joked from the back of the room. There were a few nervous giggles. Then a flash of something resembling panic passed across Goreman's face, as if he feared the joke was a prearranged signal to mutiny. His eyes darted nervously towards the exit. The panic passed in a second and he continued: "The solution, as I see it, is that all of you must work harder to see that new files are opened. The more files we open, the more difficult it will be to justify closing the office down. So I look to all of you now to make this a priority. Our mandate remains unaltered, and it is up to all of you to see that these cases, eventually, are worked up, uh, to the point that charges might be, uh, considered, and hopefully our point will be made and more funding will be . . . well . . . forthcoming."

That was it. No "Backs to the wall," no "Once more unto the breach," no "Ich bin ein Berliner." That was the beginning of the end. We never saw much of Goreman after that.

He'd stay in his office behind the door, go overseas on extended trips, attend conferences or lengthy mysterious meetings with senior bureaucrats, and generally find something to do other than deal with the matter at hand. Since he still maintained a home in Vancouver, he was known to commute back and forth on a regular basis. Needless to say, there were no more pickup games of basketball at the YMCA.

II

The task of burying the dead was hardly onerous, but notwithstanding the fact that I might very well be the last person to see these files, I felt that a certain consistency in form would be preferable. If anything, it was for the sake of posterity. I developed a format, like a kind of template, and so it became simply a matter of plugging in names, dates, places, and a few other ancillary details. I'd include some boilerplate historical background just for good measure, then wrap it all up with a few concluding lines that would leave little room for argument. The hole had already been dug, so my job was to make sure a few kind words were said before the lot was chucked in and the whole mess covered up.

Glued on the front of each file folder was a typed white label upon which was included information concerning the suspect: a full or partial name, an address, if known, and a date of birth, if known, along with a file number. The contents of each folder were secured with a clasp made of thin, malleable metal.

Some files were less substantial than others, some the mere ghosts of files, containing little in the way of an evidentiary foundation proving that the name so neatly typed on the face of the manila file belonged to one of *them*. They were rather like glimpses or shadows or fragments of tales without endings or beginnings, mere hints and bits of clues. One could draw certain inferences, make certain assumptions, but nothing more.

Others offered a bit more. I spent at least a day finishing off Erich Fehr. Fehr's name cropped up in 1989 through his wife, Anna, when an incident of marital disharmony brought the police to their Winnipeg home. Drunk and thrown out of the house, Fehr began smashing windows and destroying his wife's garden gnomes. Fehr was carted away and Anna gave a detailed statement to a young policeman describing Fehr's predilections for violence and drunken outbursts. She showed him the bruises on her arm from a previous night's attack, and these were dutifully photographed. She then made a further comment which sparked additional interest on the part of the young policeman. She told the officer that, as a young German farmer in Poland, Fehr had killed dozens of Jews with great enthusiasm after the German invasion, and that was *before* he joined the ss. She promised to provide more details if the police were interested. The officer said he would return the next evening to take down those further particulars.

What a difference a day makes. The next day Anna Fehr had a change of heart. Apparently regretting her previous candour, she told the young policeman that she no longer wished to pursue any charges against her Erich, and said that her statement was full of lies and that he had put all of those terrible words into her mouth. The cop thought enough of the incident to put every detail of the matter into the police report. He sent a copy of it along with Anna's statement to an RCMP colleague in Ottawa, who sent it on to the SPU.

The last entry in the file was dated October 1989. The young officer, who had since been transferred to the homicide unit, sent a letter advising the SPU that Fehr had been murdered by one adult and two youths who had broken into his home. He'd attached a copy of an autopsy photo that showed an SS blood-grouping tattoo found on the inside of Fehr's arm, along with a summary of the homicide report which contained this excerpt:

All three suspects were arrested within a short distance of the crime scene. One of the accused, Dwayne Mallet, later confessed to the police that he'd kicked the victim in the head until he stopped screaming. Then he and the two youths ransacked Fehr's apartment in search of money or jewellery but found neither, so Mallet said he kicked the victim in the jaw one more time and picked up a gold tooth that had popped out of Fehr's mouth. The tooth was later seized by police. Mallet told police he'd heard that the victim was an old Jew with lots of money stashed in his suite.

By 1990 suspects began to die with alarming frequency. There was little choice but to close these files, and that was anathema to Goreman's global strategy. It would be difficult in those circumstances to justify keeping a file open or to argue that there remained a reasonable prospect of conviction, but Goreman, in a moment of inspiration, came up with a rather ingenious solution. Previously, the police investigators had been randomly checking the status of all suspects to ensure that they were still alive. That was how they determined that a number of suspects had since shuffled off this mortal coil. Henceforth, Goreman decreed that no more random health checks would be conducted. In a memo addressed to all staff members he stated, "Any determination as to the life status of a suspect should not be made until charges and an arrest are ready to be effected."

Not even death would be permitted to interrupt the work of the SPU.

The weeks passed quickly. August became September, which became October, and likewise October inexorably flowed into November. All the while I laboured through the piles of brown manila until I reached the last file. *Friedrich Reile.*

It was different with Reile. I'd known this when the file first crossed my desk three years before. Now I had left that file to the last precisely because I had never ceased to forget about it. The other files could be wrapped up, shut away, and buried because most of them had never amounted to much in the first place, but that also meant that everything else that I had done here, all the work, all the time I'd invested, would come to nothing. It should have come to something. I don't know why, but it should have led somewhere instead of to this nothingness.

Reile wasn't a dream, he wasn't a rumour or a shadow. He

existed, he exists. Reile was, *is* alive, and he'd been *there*. He'd done all those things. The shootings, the gassings. I was sure of that. There had been no trial for him. He'd escaped the Soviets, he'd escaped the Germans, and now he was here, safe, in Canada. Living among us. This came as no surprise; he was in good company. There was nonetheless a process that had to be completed, a protocol to be followed. Reile had yet to pass through my hands. Then and only then would his file be closed. I had the power to put him to rest. I also had the power to cause him unrest. I'd never get a chance like this again.

It always begins and ends with a report.

FINAL REPORT

SUSPECT NAME: REILE, Friedrich
DOB: 25/March/1924
POB: Muntau, Molotschna, Tokmak District, Ukraine (Former U.S.S.R.)
CURRENT ADDRESS: 124 Elm St., Winnipeg, Manitoba
HEALTH STATUS: Surreptitious inquiries conducted by police investigators in August 1993. Subject is known to be in good health.

INTRODUCTION

The suspect was born in Muntau near Tokmak in southern Ukraine in 1924. He was an ethnic German or *Volksdeutscher*. He was fluent in both Russian and German. Muntau was located in one of the large German farming colonies in southern Ukraine at that time. Reile served as an interpreter, holding the rank of an SS man (private) with Einsatzkommando (EK) Unit 10A, which was a part of Einsatzgruppe D (EG) of the German Security Service (SD). He joined the unit sometime in early October 1941, after the German invasion of Russia (Operation Barbarossa). He remained with the unit until the fall of 1943, when it was disbanded. As an interpreter his function was to translate orders and documents. During the period of his service he actively participated in a series of mass executions of Jews and Russian citizens carried out by EK10A in regions of southern Russia: Mariupol, Taganrog, Rostov, Krasnodar, and Novorossijsk. . . .

GENERAL BACKGROUND

The suspect became a naturalized German citizen in December 1944. He remained in West Germany after the war, residing with his sister in Marburg, where he studied architecture. In 1952 he applied for a Canadian visa. He was screened and processed by Canadian vetting officers based in Karlsruhe. He was listed as a passenger on the *Dundee*, which arrived in Halifax in February 1953. In 1954 he applied for Canadian citizenship, which was granted in December of that year.

That would do for a start. I printed off a copy of these first few lines. I folded the printed pages and slipped them into a big blank envelope. I typed the address, *his address*, on the front. I felt, at that moment, like a spy or a saboteur. That was a good thing; I had begun. There was something very liberating in an action that went beyond mere thought.

SUMMARY OF FILE CONTENTS

The Reile file consists of twelve volumes of material. A summary of the contents of each volume of the file is located on the inside front cover of each volume. Volumes one, two, and three are made up of historical reports and copies of relevant documents. Volumes four to nine contain statements and court records obtained from various archives in Ukraine, Russia, and Germany relating to trials of various Einsatzgruppen personnel and collaborators. Of particular note are the trials of eleven EK10A collaborators held by the Soviets in Krasnodar in 1960-63 (ten of the eleven were executed shortly after the trial, and the eleventh was sent to a labour camp for thirty years) and the *Christmann et al.* investigations and trials carried out in West Germany in the late 1960s and early 1970s. (Christmann and a number of lesser figures were subsequently convicted and received varying jail sentences, the death penalty having been abolished previously by the West German government.)

Volumes ten and eleven contain correspondence and internal memoranda related to the handling of the file. Volume twelve contains strictly photographic evidence obtained from a variety of sources. Among them are two photographs known to be of Reile dating from the war. . . .

I picked up the photos. There was a note attached with a paper clip. It was written in longhand on an interoffice memo form. I recognized the handwriting. It was dated August 30, 1993.

MEMORANDUM

TO: Dennis Connor/file
FROM: E. Brunswick, Counsel

Dennis,
You'll remember these photos of Reile from the Landeskriminalamt, Munich. I'm also attaching some surveillance photos Gord Viaux took of our boy in Winnipeg last week at a shopping mall. Maybe Reile was doing his Christmas shopping early this year! The guy has aged pretty well, don't you think? We should all be that lucky!

Cheers,
Elizabeth

The note was neatly printed, but her signature was large in comparison, swirling, looping, as if flung onto the page.

I arranged the photographs in front of me on my desk. The first was believed to have been taken sometime in the fall of October 1941, when Reile joined EK10A. On the second photograph there was a date: "September 1942." This photograph was probably taken in Krasnodar or Rostov, as EKIOA was based in both cities around that time.

There were four additional photographs attached to a police report. They were taken surreptitiously on August 22, 1993, by Gord Viaux. I imagined his big frame stuffed into some rented compact model, his big paws fumbling with the lens cap, trying to get the damn camera into focus. Reile is walking through a row of parked cars. He has aged but he looks fit, with a full head of white hair. That was a good sign. I wanted him to be alive.

There was an extra set of the photos attached in an envelope. I took the extras and put them in the big envelope. Then I reread the note. I ran my fingers across the ink and let my fingertips rest on the name signed at the bottom.

Elizabeth.

Shit. I didn't want to see that name tonight. I had not spoken to her in eight months.

Outside my window I could see the light was beginning to fade. It was late. I sealed the envelope, put on my coat, and stuffed the envelope in one of the pockets. The streets were practically empty. The commuters, the worker bees, had fled for the day and the downtown was deserted. As I walked I felt two corners of the envelope press into my side and at once despondency welled up inside me. It was partly about her, but it was everything else, too. I walked home through a damp mist and I felt the emptiness of the night air, and the darkening sky was transformed to the colour of ash.

CHAPTER THREE

I
——

Rain turned to ice, and then became thick snow that buried
the city in blanketing layers of white, gently transforming the
shapes of objects, softening edges, leaving rounded forms and
fluffy silhouettes and covering the things that lay closest to
the ground, thereby obliterating them.

In Mariupol we took the living away to remote and lonely
pits outside the city, places cut off from the rest of the world.
We stripped them of their valuables, their clothes, and then
we took their lives as one might stamp out so many tiny
flames. We buried the dead, with sand and soil, not to honour
them, but to hide them; we used sand to conceal and to obliterate and erase them as much from our memory as from the
view of others. These horrors could be hidden and thus they
would cease to be. I watched as the HiWis shovelled sand on

the piles of bodies that lay in the ditches. At one spot a hand and part of an arm protruded a few inches above the sand. The arm wrenched one way, then another, and all the while the fingers clenched, then opened, then clenched again, as if grasping and then releasing invisible shapes in the air.

I saw Psarev, holding a shovel, stand over the hand, staring down at it. He poked at it with the tip of his shovel, dumbly, like a child jabbing with a stick at a dead sparrow or some other curious form on the ground. He let the fingers grip the edge of the shovel; then he pulled the shovel away and the hand seemed to dangle above the soil, still clutching at the air. Psarev went back to shovelling soil, piling layer upon layer until the hand and fingers were buried, disappearing into the darkness of the filled-in trench. I felt as if I had been buried there too, but by my own hand.

Another brown envelope arrived in the mail this morning. It contained another excerpt of a report. I felt that rope inside me tighten again. I smelled the stench of it again. Smoke, soil, blood. I am trapped now, in this room, in this house, in these last years of my life. *They know me. They know my name.*

I folded the papers and placed them back in the envelope. The memories of names and places washed over me.

Taganrog.

At the end of October, the main kommando moved east to Taganrog on the Sea of Azov, Zeetzen having told us that the Jewish problem in Mariupol had been resolved. As before, in

Taganrog we set up our headquarters in a school, and the interpreters were billeted together in a farm. There was a garden attached to it and a barn, too, where horses and cows were kept. A farmer from East Prussia tended to the livestock. I remember the names of the other interpreters: Richmaier, Huber, Penner, Fehr, and Fast. *Volksdeutsche*. We had changed; all of us had changed. We made up rules now, rules about conduct and speech. Certain things could not be discussed. We drank often, too. There was never any shortage of liquor, and we often guzzled the rations of vodka and schnapps. I welcomed the temporary transcendence it offered.

The kommando was continually occupied with special operations, *Aktionen*. There was so much work to be done. I did as I was told. We all did as we were told. We all did what was expected of us. Richmaier told me, when the kommando arrived in Taganrog, that there was a standing order that all members of the kommando had to participate in at least one liquidation *Aktion*, and if a man refused he would be shot. But I never heard such an order being given. Such an order was a rumour, I think. Rumour or not, I never saw anyone refuse to join the firing line. In that way we became equals: Germans, Ukrainians, Russians, *Volksdeutsche*; all of us equals now, and no one could point the finger at anyone else. I never heard such an order, but it never occurred to me to disobey.

In Taganrog, as in Mariupol, the signs and placards were posted throughout the city. "The German police organs intend to concentrate all Jews in a special district outside the city for protection. . . ." The Jewish question in Taganrog would soon be resolved.

I saw them arrive. The scene unfolded before my eyes as it would unfold so many more times. I saw old men, women and children, hundreds of them now, pushed together into a cordoned-off square. I could see their faces, marked with expressions of suspicion, distress, and growing fear. Perhaps they had heard rumours. I had begun to see them differently now. They were transformed from individual figures, from men and women, into a curious patchwork of strange creatures. They were not like me and I was not them. I stood a few metres from this teeming mass, but we were separated by the wide gulf between the living and the dead. I was still alive, but they were dead. I began to think of them now as the dead.

I was assigned to assist an SS officer named Albert Heimbach. My duty was to translate his orders so he could communicate with the HiWis and the Jews. That way there would be no confusion, no misunderstandings. I was a facilitator. I was there to make sure everything ran smoothly. The Jews had all been registered and would be divided into groups to ease their relocation. A clerk, an SS man, sat at a table and marked off the names as the line passed by and into the waiting transports. I stood with Heimbach beside the table when a young girl, the next in the line, approached. She was weeping and pleaded with the clerk, but the clerk could not understand and looked to Heimbach.

"What is she saying?" Heimbach asked me.

"She says that she is not a Jew, sir. She says that she is a Russian."

"Can you be certain of that, Reile?"

"Yes, sir, she is not a Jew. I am certain." I could tell from the way she was dressed, and from her accent when she spoke.

"Then tell her she can leave this place. She can go home. It's only the Jews that interest us now."

I told her to run away as fast as she could, and I signalled to the HiWis who guarded the perimeter of the square to let her through. She still wept, but she ran and the guards let her pass. Heimbach watched her leave. He said, "Do you know, I have two children in Berlin, twins, as young as that girl." But that was all he said.

The name of each Jew was checked off and everything was in order. Then one by one they were searched and stripped of their money, their jewels, their watches, everything that might be of value. I was ordered by Baumer, now the top sergeant, to assist in searching some of the Jews. I had done this before. We were all experienced now, and less kind than we once had been. There were so many to search and I was anxious to see the job finished, we all were: Brunschen, Baumer, Richmaier, Penner, Fehr. We all wanted this business done, and done quickly, so that the memory might somehow be diminished.

I ripped at the coat pockets of one old man. He was silent and looked down as coins, a watch, and some old medals poured out onto the pavement. Richmaier used a bayonet to slice open the linings of their coats and their jackets and their thick shirts, letting all the tiny treasures, the last little things of life, spill out onto the square. One woman screamed as he yanked at a necklace, and he slapped her across the face until she was quiet.

Some of the Jews had tried to hide their valuables in the

packages of food they'd been permitted to carry, so all the packages were yanked from their hands and thrown to the ground and dashed apart. Baumer knocked a loaf of bread from the hands of a boy and crushed it with the heel of his boot. Three small cameos had been secreted inside. The boy tried to reach for them, but Baumer grabbed him by the hair and flung him forward, causing him to tumble and skid. Then he kicked at the boy until he was able to scramble away and join the first group being loaded into the trucks.

It was early morning, yet some spectators had gathered at the other end of the square, curious, watching us, watching all of this unfold. Heimbach sent Psarev and Skripkin over to disperse them. Our actions were not to be observed.

Near Taganrog there was a place named Petruschinskaja Balka. We used it many times. It was the name of a gully that led down into a ravine, a wide and sandy pit, much deeper than the anti-tank ditches that surrounded the cities and the collective farms. The HiWis were already there when we arrived, guarding the perimeter to keep any bystanders away from the area, but we were far away from any villages or farms. Fedorov, the commander of the HiWis, stood nearby conversing with Zeetzen.

I was ordered to join the first shooting party at the edge of the ravine. A group of ten Jews had been ordered to lie face down in the ravine, and as I looked down upon them I saw steam rising from their bodies. When we fired into the bodies, sand and blood flew up into the air. Then another group of Jews was sent down into that gully and I saw them stumble and trip over the bodies that lay there. We fired again.

Heimbach said we shot four hundred that day. He was obliged to be exact. There were records that had to be kept and field reports that had to be submitted. I could not say how many were liquidated by my own hand. The balka was an unspeakable place. I saw but did not see, as if a veil had fallen across my eyes, and I was absorbed by numbness.

The winter was quite cruel, and I remained in Taganrog while a sub-kommando of twenty men was sent back to the region of Mariupol. Richmaier was among them. At the end of January 1942, he returned to Taganrog.

We sat together in a corner of the mess hall of our quarters on the second floor of the school. Richmaier cursed the cold. He was sick, he said, and could not go on like this; it was madness now, all these horrible things. He had aged in those few weeks. His skin was sallow and lined, and there was a kind of shadow behind the flesh of his face, like a blackness. He seemed smaller, frailer, like many of the others in the kommando; transformed by this life, eyes staring, blank, black; always the smell of liquor, sweet and stale, on men's breath. I felt a sickness too, deep inside me, inaccessible.

Richmaier told he that at Mariupol he had seen many Russian prisoners, too many to be cared for, so the SS came up with a solution.

"Most of the Ivans were in a bad way. They must have been captured months before and when I saw them they were very weak. They'd been held in a tractor factory. We shoved them out of there and marched them along a road towards the train station. Most of them didn't have overcoats or boots, so it was slow going and the cold was like death. We loaded them into cattle cars and then the train took off. I asked an SS man where they were being taken. He laughed and told me that there was a siding a few kilometres away, where the cars would be unhooked and left for a few days. He said the winter would take care of them after that." His voice was low when he spoke and he leaned his head forward to speak. "Some of the SS men were laughing about it. It was as if they were playing a practical joke."

Richmaier's voice was thin and soft now, his expression morose. He had always loved to talk. After this, he barely spoke at all.

II

The winter took its toll on the kommando. Diseases of all sorts had spread through our ranks: dysentery, influenza, jaundice, fevers, severe bouts of cramps, and diphtheria. Drunkenness was prevalent, more than ever before. This was not a mystery. The liquidations had continued without cease for months now. I watched the men about me crumble in their own ways. I was lucky; I suffered only from bouts of influenza, but otherwise I remained strong. I drank, though, heavily and often; but even sober I kept the cancer that festered deep within me silenced and at bay.

In August 1942 the kommando moved its headquarters to Krasnodar, a city that lay northwest of the Caucasus. We advanced behind the Wehrmacht armies that were driving eastward, thirsty for the oil fields of Baku. At Krasnodar the kommando was reinforced with a number of replacements. It was there that Zeetzen was replaced by SS Obersturmbannführer Kurt Christmann. He was a well-educated man and an avid skier. Now he was with the SS. He took command a few days after we arrived in the city. Krasnodar would serve as the base for the Hauptkommando, the centre of our operations. The region of Krasnodar,

Krasnodar Kray, was dotted with many villages and towns and smaller cities.

We were quartered in an immense seven-storey building near a bombed-out church at the corner of Sedin and Ordschonokize Streets. The building was made of concrete and brick, dirty white in colour and surrounded by barbed wire. Behind the building was a large square with a high brick wall. A ramp in the square led down to the basement and the jail cells in the bowels of this complex. The building was well known in that city because it had served as the headquarters for the Soviet Security Police, the NKVD. The Russians must have fled in great haste because some of the rooms still contained boxes of documents and files that they had failed to destroy or cart away. These were seized by the Gestapo and SD men, who occupied one of the floors of this great building. I was obliged to spend several days reading the files and translating them for the German officers. They contained lists of agents and spies, intelligence, and technical details of numerous NKVD investigations.

Christmann had brought with him a unit of thirty men known as the ski-kommando. They were Austrians and Bavarians who had been policemen before the war. They were all athletes as well, competitive skiers. Christmann had organized the unit personally, as he had coached some of the men in police sports championships before the war. I wondered why they were here, in this place, far away from snowy slopes and clean mountain air.

We had real quarters now, with real mess halls, not converted schoolrooms or dingy public halls. The night Zeetzen left, a party was held in his honour. Someone played a phonograph and there were many toasts and much drinking. That night I met one of the members of the ski-kommando, named Ulrich Holtzmann. He was very tall and lean with a kind of hangdog face and a thick jaw. He was thirty-five years old. When he smiled it was always in a grim way and there was a real toughness about him. He would need that to survive here. He said he had been an officer in Munich before the war with the criminal police. I felt very small and young in comparison to him.

"You're Reile, aren't you? One of the interpreters?" He grimaced as he drank some schnapps from his glass. "There's not a drop of beer in this whole fucking country."

Across the mess hall, Christmann was standing with some of the officers, Heimbach, Trimborn, and another named Uschan. He stood very straight, and though he was smiling, his face still seemed very tight and severe. Normally the officers drank and dined in their own mess hall, but tonight they had joined us for a toast in honour of Zeetzen.

"He's a real tough bastard," Holtzmann said, nodding in Christmann's direction. "You'll see. Tough, and a real medal chaser. He loves his ski-kommando, though. He organized it, it was all his idea. We had all skied in races before the war and we all knew Dr. Christmann. When the war started we were all going to be called up but he managed to have us recruited into the same unit. We had all the best equipment, too. Good winter wear and crampons from Innsbruck, skis from Murnau, and boots from Reiser in Munich. Christmann saw that it was all taken care of. We had five VWs ordered specially just to carry our equipment."

"Why are you here then?" I asked him.

"It's a joke," he said. "A bad joke. Our objective was to capture a meteorological station atop Mount Elbrus. There was a helluva lot of fanfare when the unit was formed. We were sent from Munich to Vienna then to Salzburg and then to Berlin. There's a photograph of us taken in Berlin being inspected by Himmler. It was summer but we were wearing white winter uniforms and caps, standing to attention with our poles and skis as if we were somewhere in the Alps. We looked ridiculous. But the SS was very proud of its ski-kommando. We were like performers in a damned circus. They wanted all of Germany to see us before we went off on our crusade."

He smiled as he spoke and seemed to relish the story, though his tone was mocking and the schnapps seemed to have warmed him to the subject.

"And now you are too late?" I said.

"Of course. The Wehrmacht beat us to it. They took the mountain while we were still rumbling across a dirt track in Ukraine. And so now, we are here in this very interesting place. I see quite a ragtag bunch here, a motley crew, I think. Wouldn't you say?"

I did not know how to reply.

"You are young man, Reile, I understand. You interpret, you follow orders, and you don't want to make any trouble for yourself. You don't have to say anything to me. I have too big a mouth, anyway. The schnapps won't help that condition."

He looked over at Christmann, who appeared to be leaving, and then he scanned the whole of the mess hall with a pair of deepset, intelligent eyes. He drained the schnapps from his glass and grabbed the bottle to pour again. He nodded at me while he held the bottle.

"Yes," I said. He filled my glass to the brim, then filled his own.

"My brother-in-law was a tanker in the ss. He's back in Munich now. His leg is smashed but he's alive. I used to visit him in the hospital before I left Munich. He told me about some of the things that he had seen in Russia. He told me about these kommandos, the Einsatzkommandos, like this one I'm sure. He told me things; his mouth is as big as mine. It is an offence to talk about such matters, but his leg is smashed. Why should he care? They can do nothing more to him now."

"What did he say?" I asked.

He was quite serious now. He looked down at his glass and adjusted it with his fingers, sliding it back and forth across the wooden table, like a chess piece moved from square to square and back again. He didn't lower his voice and he didn't seem to care if anyone overheard him.

"He told me that I would be quite busy in my new kommando, and that I wouldn't likely be doing much in the way of skiing."

"I think your brother-in-law is right," I said.

He gave me one of his grim smiles. "For an interpreter, you're pretty careful with your words."

I was careful, but only to preserve my own mental state. It was easier if one simply didn't talk about the duties we performed.

He emptied his glass in one swallow and filled it again with more of the clear liquid from the bottle. "Not a fucking beer to be had in this fucking country. By the way," he added, "we've brought you a doctor."

Goertzen, "Doctor" Goertzen, had arrived with the ski-kommando. He was an SS Sturmführer, a junior officer in the kommando. He did not have the bearing of a soldier. He seemed very ill at ease in a uniform, clumsy, awkward. His hair was very blond, almost white, and the shape of his nose made me think of a pig. He seemed an outsider, even amongst his fellow officers. Holtzmann said he was a horse doctor and the nickname stuck.

Under Christmann the kommando was reorganized into several sub-units that we called vorkommandos or teilkommandos. These units were then sent out for days and weeks to the outlying villages and towns: north to Jejsk, east to Anapa, to Novorossijsk, and to the shores of the Black Sea. Most of the ski-kommando men were sent to Temruk. I watched these units leave the courtyard, sent off in the transport trucks, the officers following in cars or smaller vehicles called *Kübelwagen*. Sometimes the gas vans would accompany them. Richmaier told me they were well known even to the citizens in Krasnodar now, with the windows still painted on as a disguise. They called them black ravens.

I remained in Krasnodar with the hauptkommando. It was autumn, and the days were indistinguishable from one another. The Jewish population of Krasnodar had been registered and many were regularly collected from their homes and taken to the cellar of our headquarters. Each morning was the same. While it was still dark I was sent down to the cells to rouse the prisoners. The HiWis acted as escorts and the Jews were marched along a corridor to the ramp that led up to the courtyard. The gas vans could hold as many as sixty people. I watched as the prisoners were crammed into those black trucks. It seemed as if there would never be an end to this. Then the back door of the truck was sealed shut and it would travel along a special route to the outskirts of the city.

Brunschen once told me that it took seventeen minutes to do the job properly, though they would take twenty minutes to be safe. He said that there were many places outside Krasnodar where the trucks could be unloaded: ravines and anti-tank ditches and wells where the bodies were regularly dumped and buried. Sometimes I had to go along, but I always remained in the front with the driver. The awful work of unloading was always left to the HiWis. I would hear the banging and scraping sounds coming from the back of the van and I heard the sounds of coughing and retching. The smell was there, too, carbon monoxide. But I stayed in the front cab so I would not have to see that work being done.

In October, the ski-kommando returned. I was sent out with them on what was to be a large operation commanded by Christmann. Holtzmann was there with two other Bavarians, Hans Nachtigal and Werner Hoelst. Holtzmann and Nachtigal had been promoted to sergeant after *Aktionen* against some partisans near Temruk. I rode with them in the transport and

Christmann led the convoy in his car. This was to be an anti-partisan operation, but that could mean many things. I had been on such operations before and often they had little to do with partisans.

As we drove out of Krasnodar, Holtzmann began to shout so he could be heard above the noise of the truck. His voice was deep and gruff. These months had made him seem tougher even than before, when I first met him. But like the rest of us, he looked very tired now, and the lines around his eyes seemed deeper.

"Partisans! Where are all these partisans? I've seen none, just these wretched Jews. There seems to be no end to them." He coughed and spat out the back of the truck. "I am tired of this shitty work. We stink, all of us, stink of death."

Nachtigal sat slumped in one corner of the back of the transport, squat, stocky, wide-faced, with a head planted firmly into his shoulders. He was sick, not simply from drinking too much the night before, but diseased, I think, jaundice or dysentery perhaps. His skin was sallow, almost yellowed, with black shadows below his cheeks and beneath his eyes touches of grey, too, and beads of sweat around his temples and along his forehead. "Shut up, you piece of shit," he said. "You talk so much. No one wants to hear your stupid chatter, you just make it worse for us. The sooner this is all done, the sooner we are rid of this shit-hole."

"Don't bark at me, you stinking pig," said Holtzmann. "You're right, I should be grateful to serve the Fatherland as a butcher." His eyes shone, his jaw jutting forward, and then he looked at me. "You know, Reile, you should have been with us in Temruk. You'd have plenty of medals on your chest now. Christmann made us sergeants because we filled so many ditches with Jews and some starved bastards we'd rounded up who'd been hiding in the forests since the winter. Hey, Nachtigal! If you survive the day, you can go back to Munich soon and tell your wife about all the partisans you killed. You can show her your medals. She'll be very proud, I'm sure. Then she'll stop screwing those SS staff officers who always seem to be on leave. What will you tell her, though, about what you did in the war?"

"Stinking swine." Nachtigal tried to get up, but just as he did the truck jolted to a sudden stop and he fell forward, flat onto the bed of the truck, his carbine rattling against the steel floor as it fell from his hands. Holtzmann moved forward to help him but he shook him off. "Get away, you piece of shit." Nachtigal struggled to his feet. It was apparent that he was in pain.

"You should go see the horse doctor," Holtzmann laughed, sitting back down.

Nachtigal got to his feet and then moved to the back of the truck where he slumped down awkwardly, wiping some sweat from his eyes. "Goertzen is not a doctor, he's a butcher," he said. "Hoelst told me he took his medical studies in Poland but he never attained a degree. He's only good for prowling the ditches to decide who's dead and who isn't. But I don't think he has the belly to shoot. He'd rather have others pull the trigger."

Our truck had not moved since it had jolted to a halt and sent Nachtigal careering forward. Then we heard the sharp, harsh voice that we knew was Christmann's. Holtzmann yelled at us all to get out of the truck. I heard shots being fired, and my heart lurched. I thought it was an ambush.

I had started to follow Holtzmann out of the truck when I heard another volley, and the crackling sounds of sporadic shots being fired. I jumped down from the transport and dashed around the truck in pursuit of Holtzmann. Our convoy had stopped on a dirt track that bordered a great flat farm field; perhaps wheat or barley had been grown here, but now it was barren and black, though the winter was still weeks away.

I saw Christmann as I ran to the front of the truck. He wore the black uniform of the ss, with high boots and a slouched cap with a peak. By now he was standing outside of his car and looking in the direction of that wide field. He told Holtzmann to get all the men out of the trucks and Holtzmann ran back to the transports yelling out orders.

Then Christmann looked at me and said, "You, come with me." I followed him out into that field of black soil towards a group of shooters who had formed a line some one hundred yards away.

Christmann. I see him still. But what can I write of him now? Blue, cold eyes. A thin, clipped moustache. A face that was taut, angled, severe, a look of such darkness, but not an evil face, not the face of evil, but a face that knew evil, that had seen evil. He was staring straight ahead at the group of shooters who had yet to notice our approach. I looked back and saw the kommando men scrambling out of the trucks, following us, but they were still many yards behind.

A group of Ukrainian policemen were standing about in the open field. Their uniforms were dirty and their tunics open at the front. As we approached I understood why I had heard the shooting. Ten yards in front of the Ukrainians there was a group of about forty Jews. I had seen this so many times now, the huddled, naked bodies, the dead not yet dead. And yet this was different, because they stood on a patch of ground that was littered with the bodies of others, some still alive, writhing, trembling, arms or legs thrashing and flailing about. Towards the west, in full view of the Ukrainians, there was a collective farm and an orchard. The women in the orchard had stopped working and were staring at the policemen.

One of the policemen walked amongst the bodies, slamming the butt of his rifle down on the ones that showed signs of life. Then he walked back and joined the rest of the policemen. Another began to fire, the bullets smashing the knee and thigh of an old man, spinning him up into the air and then down. The others laughed and then began to take turns, firing one or two shots at random, then stopping for a while. Their shooting was wildly inaccurate.

They did not see Christmann until he was upon them. His voice was full of rage as he yelled out in German, demanding who was in command. I quickly translated for him, trying my best to sound as fierce, but the Ukrainians stood there dumbly, looking at me with indifference, until one man stepped forward, a police captain, who said that he was in command. He held a bottle in his hand and staggered as he walked. His face was red and blotchy and I could smell the liquor that wafted from the shiny film of sweat smeared across his brow.

"Who ordered this operation?" Christmann demanded.

The police captain said his orders came from Krasnodar, from the SD. I translated for Christmann and added, "I think they're all drunk, sir."

Then the captain turned his back on Christmann and shouted to his men to form a line and finish the job.

Christmann did not wait for my translation, he did not wait for a single word. In the moment it took for the police captain to turn his back, Christmann had his pistol out of its holster and the barrel was now pressed hard into his temple. The captain froze; he must have felt the barrel pressed hard into the side of his head, the finger on the trigger. Christmann's face was like stone, and his eyes dark now, like a blackness, his countenance like a terror.

"Tell him I am the commander of the SD in this region and if he does not order his men to retire I shall put a bullet through his brain. Tell him!"

The police captain did as he was ordered and the Ukrainians began to fall back, sullen, staggering, stupid, and drunk. They walked from us towards the orchard where the women still stood and watched. Christmann stared at them and spat as he put his pistol back in the holster. "Filth," Christmann said. "Human filth."

By now the other kommando men had caught up to us and the group of still-living Jews stood a few yards away, silent, staring at all of this, alone in that empty field. The body of the old man was still now, a heap on the ground, one arm bent upwards in a peculiar way. He lay near other heaps, bloodied, twisted up in the soil.

Christmann snapped his head towards Holtzmann, who was standing beside him. "Load them." He pointed to those naked souls a few yards away. "Load them into one of the transports and get them out of here. The bodies, too."

"There are anti-tank ditches dug two kilometres east of here, sir," said Holtzmann, breathing hard from running across the field. Nachtigal was still struggling to catch up to where we stood.

"Take them there, then," Christmann said. "I want this mess put to an end."

III

In November 1942, I was ordered to accompany Heimbach and Goertzen and a company of HiWis to a municipal hospital just east of the city. We left Krasnodar in the morning and two gas vans lumbered behind us. The roads were terrible, dirt tracks turned to muck, and it took hours to complete the journey. I discovered that the hospital was a sprawling complex painted white. It had an annex, which Goertzen explained to me was a sanatorium for the deformed and the mentally ill. We were met outside the main building by a nurse and a doctor wearing white smocks. I gathered that they were expecting us. I stood there with Heimbach and Goertzen, and Heimbach told me to ask them where the children's ward was. The doctor pointed to the annex entrance a few yards to the right and said, "There." I translated Heimbach's orders to the HiWis and the Ukrainian policemen and they walked as a group towards the door at the front of the annex. One of the gas vans was driven over to the same door. The nurse pointed to the gas van and whispered something to the doctor.

Heimbach must have heard her speak. "What did she say?" he asked me sharply.

"*Dushegubka*," I said, looking at Heimbach. "It means soul-destroyer."

Heimbach looked at the nurse, who seemed quite afraid. She was trembling. But Heimbach's voice was soft now. "Tell her that . . ." His voice trailed off and I stared at him, waiting for him to finish, but he looked away, towards the annex.

"Tell her we will be quick," Goertzen said, while Heimbach walked away.

After a few minutes I saw the Ukrainians carrying the children out. I asked the doctor what was wrong with the patients. He said that some of the children were mongoloid, others hydrocephalic. The Ukrainians carried them like little sacks over their shoulders. I saw one child struggling, making horrible, incomprehensible shrieks, but most were simply silent. Psarev was leading two young girls by the hand; they were perhaps five years old. Psarev seemed to be joking with them because they were giggling and smiling. All the while he moved them along and then helped them up into the back of the gas van gently, as if they were his own. When the gas van was filled, Goertzen gave the order to seal the back door. Then I heard the frantic banging from within after the door was secured. Goertzen waved at the driver and the van pulled away.

Goertzen had changed, though. The horse doctor was now quite nervous, distracted, and his voice shook as he gave the orders to start rounding up the adult mental patients, schizophrenics mostly, from the other ward. I translated the orders and the HiWis did as they were told. Goertzen was trembling a little as I translated his orders, and he appeared to be struggling to maintain his composure. I realized this must have been his first euthanasia *Aktion*. I thought of telling him that he would find it would all become easier with time, but he would have thought me impertinent since I was only an interpreter. Heimbach stood a few yards away, as if pretending to be divorced from it all.

Heimbach did not speak to me of his children in Berlin that day. Perhaps they were too far away.

We lost Baumer shortly after Christmas, 1942. Brunschen told me about it as we were sitting in one of the gas vans parked in the courtyard at the headquarters in Krasnodar, waiting for Fedorov and his men. The truck generated little heat and we sat there huddled down, our breath frail, opaque puffs of white. Brunschen told me that one of the gas vans had become stuck in the snow on one of the roads in Krasnodar. It had simply been left there by one of the Russian HiWis who had been driving it. Brunschen found out and immediately told Baumer, who was furious. He and Brunschen drove to the spot and found the truck sitting at a slant, with two of its wheels off the road and lodged in a wide drift of snow. The truck was too heavy to push because it was crammed full of bodies.

"The cold was like death. We tried to drag out some of the bodies, but they were frozen in place, all tangled together as hard as concrete," Brunschen said. "Then Baumer began screaming. He pushed me out of the truck and began kicking at the bodies, ordering them to get up. Penner was there too, and so Baumer told him to translate his orders. Penner tried to say that it was no use, they were all dead, but Baumer would have none of it. He kept kicking at the bodies and screaming, 'Raus! Raus! Filthy bastards, get up! I decide who lives and dies!' He pulled out his pistol and began firing down into some of the corpses. The bullets made horrible sounds when they tore into the frozen corpses. Then he jumped out of the van and kept screaming at me and Penner, saying, 'Look, see the bodies all around us now, on the road, in the snow, in the doorways, hanging from the windows, do you see them?' But of course there were none to be seen, just the frozen bodies in that black van."

I remembered Baumer at the *Aktion* in Mariupol, just some fourteen months before, grey-faced, sweating, but in control, yelling orders, telling everyone to move quickly.

Brunschen said that fortunately some of the ski-kommando men arrived, Holtzmann and Nachtigal and Hoelst, and they tackled Baumer and took away his pistol. "Otherwise I'm sure he would have put a bullet in his own brain." He sounded relieved when he said this. But I thought they should have let him shoot himself; that would have been the kindest thing to do. Instead Baumer was sent home to Germany, for good, to a military hospital, and I wondered if he still saw the bodies lying all around him.

We heard Fedorov's Russians and Ukrainians arrive in a transport truck that drove into the courtyard. I opened the large doors to the cellar and went down the ramp. Brunschen and I ordered the Jews out of the cells. Most of them were young women who had worked at a collective farm near the city. They had been lying together to keep warm, but they did as they were ordered and we sent them up the ramp and into the courtyard where the gas vans were waiting.

Usually the vans were backed right up to the entrance of the basement, but Fedorov ordered them farther away from the door. This meant that each woman would have to run a gauntlet formed by some of Fedorov's men. None of the women had any shoes and their clothes were soiled, like rags. As they scrambled towards the trucks the Ukrainians pushed them to the ground and poked them with the barrels of their rifles. One woman, her hair shorn for lice, was struck across the face with a gun barrel, and blood began to stream down her face. "Don't worry, we are taking you to the showers," a Russian said. "We are going to make you very clean today."

One month later Christmann announced that the Sixth Army had surrendered in Stalingrad, which meant that the front was collapsing and the kommando would be forced to evacuate Krasnodar. There was no panic, but time was nevertheless of the essence. Rumours circulated that the Russians were only a few kilometres from Krasnodar, though this was not true. Nevertheless, all documents, all records, all intelligence reports were gathered up and burned. We were obliged to travel light now.

After the building was emptied, the kommando assembled in the courtyard and we were loaded into our transport trucks. The basement was filled with mines and firebombs that would be detonated once we left. We drove away in a column. Holtzmann and Nachtigal were left behind to finish the job before rejoining our column. Minutes later I heard a series of crackling explosions as the mines and bombs were detonated. Richmaier and Fehr were seated beside me in the truck, and when we heard the explosions in the distance, Richmaier told me in a lowered voice that the cells in the basement had still been filled with prisoners. He had helped carry the mines and firebombs into the basement.

"The cells were stuffed with prisoners, Jews, partisans, commissars. We rigged the bombs all around the cells and they watched us." His voice was flat, lifeless when he spoke. Fehr was silent.

I said that we were well rid of this place, and no one replied.

We drove out of Krasnodar along a wide boulevard. Dozens of bodies were strung by their necks from a row of lampposts that bordered both sides of the boulevard. Richmaier pointed at one of the corpses as we passed. "Last night," he said. "Fedorov's work." He said that they were probably partisans or suspected spies rounded up in the last few days by Fedorov's men.

The column halted outside the city. Holtzmann's crew caught up to us. The black smoke from our headquarters rose from the centre of the city. We headed southwest to Novorossijsk, where we were to be evacuated.

I remember that someone took photographs. I think it was when the kommando was in Novorossijsk. Such things were forbidden, but in spite of this some of the men had smuggled cameras along with them. This was the first time that I ever remembered seeing anyone take a photograph. We had been loaded onto two wide barges that would take us across the Black Sea to the Crimea. There were five of us who sat in wooden chairs at a small table. Holtzmann, Richmaier, Fehr, and Penner. Bottles of wine were opened and were passed around. We drank the wine out of tin cups and we posed for the photograph with our arms around each others' shoulders, our tin cups raised in a toast. We were smiling and laughing, even Richmaier, who I thought was at the end of his rope. I don't know how we could all smile like that. We smiled in spite of ourselves, we smiled because we made ourselves forget, even if only for the second it took to snap that photograph. But after our time in Krasnodar we were, all of us, capable of anything.

As we crossed the open water I remember the wind whipping against my face and the smell of the sea as we drank the wine. I felt my insides soften and swell with the warmth of the liquor, as if I was becoming human again.

I walked away from the others to the pilot's cabin and stood beside him. He was very talkative, spoke to me in Russian, and told me to look towards the north. I peered in that direction, using my hand to shade my eyes a little from the bright sun. The barge ploughed through waters that were rollicking and dark, but to the north the waters were brighter and calmer and unmistakably blue. "Azov," the pilot said. "The Sea of Azov. Where the black meets the blue."

Across the water, on the other side of those blue waters, he told me that there was a port named Taganrog where he had been born. "I have been away for many years, but as a child I remember it was very pretty. There is a house there where Chekhov was born. Do you know it?"

I told him that I had never been there.

I

At first I hesitated, uncertain how to move. Then the idea came to me in an idle moment as I sat alone in the coffee room and ruminated over a cigarette, feeling the acrid roughness of the smoke rush across the back of my throat. I remembered a line from a poem that I thought I had forgotten, about being "pinned and wriggling" and unsure about how to begin. I felt pinned and wriggling now, unable to move forward or back. I wondered if I could stay here forever in this tiny room, this time capsule on the sixth floor, preserved in crystal or dry ice, with my coffee and cigarettes and the increasing weight of my own frustration.

What kind of man had *he* become, this Reile? Was he haunted by the past? Were there demons that visited him in his dreams? I could not know. I hoped the letters and the photos might elicit some response. I didn't know what the effect would be. But it was the *not* knowing that made it interesting, like throwing a stone down a well and waiting to hear the splash. It wasn't a prank, it wasn't a joke. Something had to be done, and it was the best that I could come up with; it was all that I *could* do. This was the most that anyone *had* done. No convoluted process, no lengthy trial, no pompous lawyers with their obfuscating ways, their prevaricating rhetoric, their sophistry and syllogistic fraud.

I sent Reile two photos and a few words on a page, just in case he thought we'd forgotten all about him.

He lived. I was sure of that. Viaux's photos offered a good indication that Reile would be around for a while. He lived in spite of his past. One day the killing ended, just as suddenly as it must have begun. Then he moved on, as everyone else moved on.

Some things are just too easy.

I called the directory-assistance operator in Winnipeg, and indeed there was a telephone listing for an F. Reile of 124 Elm Street in River Heights. The last health-status check had been conducted by Viaux almost a year before, and it seemed that Reile was at that time still in good health. He was seventy years of age and the photographs made him look ten years younger. I just knew that Reile was not the type to die young.

Before Goreman had proscribed health checks, the police at the SPU would regularly call suspects pretending to be insurance salesmen or telemarketers or government employees seeking to update their records. The ruse rarely failed. Old people, even old Nazis, can be very trusting. Viaux told me that sometimes when he made these calls he couldn't get off the line.

"Once they start talking," he said, "you can't get them to shut up."

They were likely surprised to learn that anyone still cared.

The worst that could happen was that he would hang up on me, so I had nothing to lose. I cultivated a tone that was slightly officious, sufficiently disinterested, and a touch patronizing, so that Reile could have no doubt that I was who I claimed to be: a functionary with the civil service, grey, nameless, with a slight chip on one shoulder and a heightened sense of self-entitlement.

I said my name was Mr. Frayer (it would be Dave, should he press the matter) with the Records Department of the Directorate of Revenue and Income; I said that the Directorate was converting all its files and the files of its clients (clients sounded better than taxpayers, more voluntary perhaps) to a new computer database (god knows what that meant).

"We need to update some of our information, Mr. Reilly . . ." (*the pretence of an error, a nice touch, suggestive of apathy, and a healthy measure of official incompetence. Very convincing*).

"It's Reile, not Reilly. I'm not Irish, I'm German." *His voice.* A little guarded. A little hostile. Yet soft-sounding, a slight rasp betraying his age, a thick accent betraying his past.

"Oh yes, quite, I'm sorry. I'll change that. Anyway, in short, we just want to know if you are still alive" (touch of impertinence now – he'll take me for an officious little prick who resents even having to make these calls).

There was a pause on the other end of the line – damn, too fucking clever – but then he chuckled and assured me that he was very much alive, that he still lived in the same house he'd lived in for twenty-five years. He said that he was alone now since his wife died last year. He would stay in the house, he said, as long as he was still able to care for his garden, but he'd had trouble with all the leaves this year and a nice young man from the next house had offered to help . . . and so on and so on. . . . Viaux was right: these people just won't quit once you get them started. I had to cut him off; I couldn't appear to be too interested.

"Well, that's fine, Mr. Reile, thank you for your time, sir." Viaux would have been proud.

A few days later I sent the photos and that first excerpt from my report. That was the first shot across the bow. I thought about wearing gloves when I handled the photographs, or signing the letters with a false name, or routing the mail through another city. In the end I just shoved the envelope in a mailbox without putting a return address on the back. He'd know the city from the postmark on the envelope, but that didn't identify the sender. He might guess who had sent it, he might figure it out. But in the end, who was he going to complain to?

I used my computer to cut and paste, and printed out another excerpt from my report. I grabbed a blank envelope and shoved the papers into it. It looked quite convincing, with all the authority of the typed word on the page.

SYNOPSIS OF INDIVIDUAL EKIOA OPERATIONS

The German invasion of the Soviet Union was initially successful. Following in the wake of the Wehrmacht and Waffen-SS divisions in all theatres of the Eastern Front were mobile killing units known as the Einsatzgruppen (EG), made up of members of the German Security Police (SiPo) and Security Service (SD). There were four EGs: A, B, C, and D, each the approximate size of a battalion. EG A was based in the Baltic region, EG B in Byelorussia, EG C in northern Ukraine, and EG D in the region immediately north of the Black Sea, eventually moving south into the region of the Caucasus. Each EG was in turn divided into smaller units of approximately 100 to 120 men known as Einsatzkommandos (EKs). These units operated throughout the newly occupied territories, either as a full unit or as sub-units known as Sonderkommandos or Teilkommandos. Existing original documents state that the primary function of the EGs was to locate and exterminate commissars and spies, and to protect ethnic German (*Volksdeutsche*) communities located in southern Ukraine. Any written orders pertaining to their primary function, the extermination of the Jewish population, were purposely euphemistic or vague. In addition, killing operations were carried out, where possible, in remote or cordoned-off locations so as not to draw attention to the mass executions. . . .

The EKs relied upon the support of members of the local population. Units of Russians, Ukrainians, Cossacks, etc. were formed and attached to the EK units. They were known as Hilfeswillige or HiWis (helpers). Local police forces were also enlisted to assist the EKs in some executions.

SYNOPSIS OF INDIVIDUAL EK10A OPERATIONS (cont'd)

MARIUPOL

Einsatzkommando 10 arrived in Mariupol in mid-October 1941. The kommando was still commanded by Colonel Heinz Zeetzen at that time. (He was replaced by Kurt Christmann on July 13, 1942.) After the arrival of the kommando, the Jewish population was ordered to collect at an assembly place near a central location in the city. They were then transported by the kommando trucks to a group of anti-tank ditches located about eight kilometres outside of the city. The city was also searched to ensure that no Jews remained in hiding.

The executions were carried out over a period of about three days. Eight thousand Jews were executed here. Numerous witness statements confirm that all members of EK10 participated in the executions. All members were ordered to take part in the *Aktion* without exception. According to the statement of EK10 member Richmaier, an ethnic German interpreter who was tried and executed by the Soviets in 1963, he observed the suspect Reile at the execution site and believed that he saw him standing at the edge of the anti-tank ditch translating the orders of the German officers, telling groups of Jews to stand in a line beside a trench. He stated that he saw Reile firing into the bodies of the Jews with a pistol. Richmaier claimed to have observed the executions from a distance as he was guarding the cordon. He denied taking any active part in this execution. (See Appendix "DD," Soviet Investigation Statements: Statement of S. Richmaier, 8/3/61.)

Richmaier remained with the kommando throughout its operations in Mariupol, Taganrog, Rostov, and Krasnodar. As stated above, he was among a group of eleven former EK10 members prosecuted by the Soviet Procurator in Krasnodar in 1963. The others tried were a mixture of ethnic Germans and Ukrainians and Russians who had collaborated with EK10. Ten of the eleven were executed shortly after being convicted. The eleventh, Valentin Sikorenko, was sentenced to thirty years of hard labour. Sikorenko provided several statements incriminating Reile. He claimed to have known Reile and to have seen him participate in a series of mass executions of Jews and other Russian citizens in the regions of the cities of Krasnodar and Novorossijsk in the fall of 1942. EK10 was based in Krasnodar at that time. . . .

Russian authorities have confirmed that Sikorenko is alive and in good health and able to be interviewed by Canadian authorities. It is expected that he will cooperate as a witness in any proceedings launched against Reile. . . .

I reread the excerpt and deleted the references to Richmaier's death. Reile didn't need to know that. Why give away so much? And it was important for Reile to believe *he* was still a going concern, to have no idea that in fact his story lay dormant in a file that was soon to be sealed away. I sent the package three weeks after I'd mailed the previous envelope. I wanted Reile to have time to mull things over. It's always worse when things unravel at a slow pace.

II

This morning my computer screen told me it was December 2, 1994, I had no reason to quarrel with it. It's very quiet here now. There are only a few of us left: a couple of historians hired for a six-month term to help me close the remaining files, two secretaries to see that everything is bundled up and sent off to wherever it is that bundled-up files are supposed to be laid to rest.

From time to time Goreman would poke his head in to see how things were winding up. He seemed a little relieved to see that the stacks of files in my office were diminishing with each of his visits. Indeed, those visits, never frequent, always brief, were few and far between in October and November. The last time I saw him was this last week when he came to say goodbye. He told me that he was soon going back to Vancouver with the Directorate of Regulations. Actually, it wasn't exactly in Vancouver, but somewhere close by, he said. He was a little evasive on that point and I didn't wish to pry. I did not particularly care. As I recall, it had something to do with fisheries.

I was now in the habit of coming in to work late in the morning and staying until past midnight. It was easier than going home and sitting about my empty apartment.

Sometimes, when the back of my neck ached from being hunched over the computer, I'd go for a stroll, taking the long way down the four-cornered hallway that followed the length and width of the sixth floor in order to reach the kitchen known as the coffee room and fix myself a mug of that bile. I had experimented with a number of coffee brands and filters, and had even brought my own high-tech coffee maker (white, with a rounded design, and made by Germans), but the result was always the same: bitter and black, like certain brands of medicated dandruff shampoo. I think the light and the air in this place turned everything sour.

I would meander back to my office, sometimes pausing in the library, in the alcove where Viaux had worked, in the document room still filled with boxes of papers where the translators and research assistants had laboured: labelling, noting, recording, organizing the hundreds of thousands of papers that came through. I'd stand for a moment in the coveted corner office, which seemed even roomier now that Goreman's furnishings had been removed, and I could stare at the lights and the buildings of the empty downtown. I was like the owner of a house who, having sold the place and moved his possessions, spends a few last minutes in each empty room, performing tiny obsequies to the memory of that house, his heart tinged with sadness and regret.

I noticed that the name-plates on the walls beside the offices of the lawyers and historians still remained, as if in expectation that everyone would soon return. They were made of plastic and could be easily removed and replaced. Around this place, that was a very practical feature. Towards the end, no one bothered to remove them when someone left. I read one of the names as I walked: *Digby Hunt*. His office had been next to Goreman's, a little way down the hall. Next was mine and then, farther down, Elizabeth's. *Elizabeth Brunswick*. I ran my fingers across the plate and let my fingertips follow the grooves of the letters of her name engraved in the plastic. I removed the name-plate from the wall and stuck it in my pocket. I stood in the hallway with my eyes closed, absolutely still. She had stood here, right on this spot, right before me where I now stood, but it was as if she had never been here. All that I could see of her now was that plastic name-plate. People come and go. That's simply the way it is.

I went home later that night as I did every night. I was sleepwalking through life these days, numb and cold all at once, unconnected, so detached from everything but those precious files. I took the name-plate home, another souvenir of the past.

Another excerpt, another envelope:

EK10A OPERATIONS IN AND AROUND KRASNODAR

In August 1942 EK10A advanced into the Caucasus region. The main kommando (Hauptkommando) set up its headquarters in Krasnodar, where they remained until February 1943. Sub-units of EK10A (Sonderkommandos and Teilkommandos) were sent to outlying cities and towns such as Novorossijsk, Jejsk, Anapa, and Temruk, and other areas. Executions were carried out regularly throughout these regions. For example, during this period, it is estimated that units of EK10A in the Rostov area alone liquidated approximately 7,000 Jews, in addition to partisans, Communists, and commissars. Of note was a mass execution of 2,000 Jews at a collective farm near Rostov in the summer of 1942.... According to KGB documents and independent West German investigation reports, ethnic German interpreters actively participated in these killings, as did the collaborating units of HiWis....

I had begun to close in.

III

Digby Hunt began work at the SPU in 1991, shortly after Horvat was indicted. Digby had hair that was dark and thick, and very straight. It defied even the most glutinous hair product by refusing to stay down or obey the force of gravity. As he read through his files looking for names and statements, hoping for the breakthrough that might see him at last enter the doors of a courtroom, he'd run his hands through his hair, tugging it, twirling it, picking at a patch of his scalp just above his left ear. I don't think he even knew he was doing it. Sometimes I'd go into his office to fetch him for coffee in the late afternoon and he'd appear quite mad, trying to read while his eyes were red and squinty from the aridity of the sixth floor and the dim light, his hair completely on end, like tall grass on a prairie.

Digby had a very pleasant face, not distinguished or chiselled, but not featureless either. As he worked away on his files, tugging away at his hair, his mouth and jaw would often appear tightly set and a frown would ripple across his brow in an expression of quiet determination. "It's all here, Dennis," he'd say, pointing to his files set out flat on the long shelves of his bookcase, like casserole dishes at a smorgasbord. "If we look long enough, we'll find the witnesses, because there *are* witnesses, and we'll find that some of them are still alive."

Digby was a journeyman, not an ace, not a star, but the pleasant chap who would keep banging his head against the wall until someone told him to stop. He simply didn't understand that time was not on his side. Time worked against so many things. It obliterated, it despoiled, it ruined all the good things. Though for some, those lucky few, that secret band of guilty brothers, time was always on their side.

Sometimes we would take a stroll in the afternoon sun down Sparks Street Mall to browse. It was a bit of a wasteland now: bookstores closing, replaced by chains and franchises, trashy eateries and bars with names like Tooters or Bobby D's. By mid-afternoon, Digby's hair would be irretrievably messy and the top button of his shirt undone.

I was no sartorial wizard myself, my wardrobe consisting of racks of tweedy blazers, pullovers, and pants of brown or blue corduroy. Digby wore a much finer cut of cloth, but it was wasted upon him. I suspect that Bryndyce did the shopping, as the styles and the labels of his suit and shirts looked foreign. European, no doubt. I suspected she dressed him each morning. He'd be at work by nine looking well pressed, tied up, buttoned up, with his hair set in order and properly restrained. But like a patched leak that won't stop seeping or a cropped weed that always grows back, an unseen and mysterious force, perhaps the paranormal or a magic goat, would undo all of Bryndyce's work in a matter of a few hours or less. Creases would form where no creases ought to be, stains would appear without a hint to their origin, and by three in the afternoon Digby's Italian suits would resemble relief maps of Alpine regions and his silk ties would be reduced to loose hankies wrapped around his neck. I would appear natty in comparison.

When Goreman was assigned the Horvat case, he requested that Digby act as his junior counsel, and Digby was happy to oblige. Goreman knew a journeyman when he saw one. He told Digby he'd need someone to carry his bags and briefcases and take care of all the legal research. Digby took that to be a compliment. But who could blame him? This was Digby's first trial.

Previous to his being hired by the SPU, Digby had been counsel to the Board of Regulatory Drafting (BORD) for two years. It was all pretty dry stuff, he said, slow death. He'd show up in the morning and proofread drafts of regulations until someone woke him up at four-thirty and let him go home. Digby said he couldn't go back to that kind of life. He wanted to be a litigator, he wanted to see action in a court-room. "Otherwise," he said, "it is back to the morgue."

After the ignominy of the Horvat trial there was a mourning period of sorts. Digby took the defeat quite hard and disap-peared for a two-week holiday, which he hoped would leave him feeling reinvigorated. He looked quite tired when I saw him in the hallway his first day back. He'd put on weight. He saw my eyes glide down towards his midriff. One of the lower buttons of his shirt was undone and a little tuft of black belly-button hair was peeking out.

"I know," he said. "I gained eight pounds. I was hoping to lose ten, but I couldn't exercise."

"What happened? I thought you were going to take a break, play some squash, that sort of thing."

"Not much of a holiday," he sniffed. "Bryndyce's friends, Gretchen and Karl, from Switzerland dropped by, unannounced, uninvited, for three days, and stayed two weeks. You should have seen them, backpacker types, kind of dirty-looking, Green Party acolytes and looking sullen all the time. Gretchen never shaved her armpits or legs and never wore a bra . . ."

I had an image of a lithe athletic Alpine beauty, with milky white skin, flimsy cotton T-shirt, and such breasts as few mortals had beheld. I raised my brows at Digby to suggest that this sounded like a good thing. He noted my renewed interest but quickly dispelled the delightful erotic thoughts that had been prancing unrestrained through the Alpine meadow I'd imagined in my brain.

"She was *not* alluring," he told me. "She was sort of floppy and hairy with a kind of film covering her. Karl never shaved, either, nor seemed to wash, *anything*. He just looked sulky and disdainful."

I rolled my eyes. I hated them now, too, if only to hop on Digby's bandwagon. I was also angry at Gretchen for spoiling my fantasy and not being blonde and gorgeous with angelic breasts.

"Sort of Euro-trash?" I asked.

"Not exactly. It was all an affectation. Each of them has parents in Zurich who are loaded and gave them the cash to come over here for a couple of months, presumably hoping they'd join a commune or something and never return. They blew the money and said they hated Canada: no trains, too cold, terrible coffee, and the discos closed too early. They kept saying they wished they had gone to America instead."

"Why did they come to visit then?"

"Bryndyce said they had been close friends since she was a teenager who just wanted to see her, but I think they were just out of money and our house was as far as they got before they had to go back home. I dumped them at the airport this morning and came straight here."

"I hate the Swiss," I said, for no particular reason, but it felt liberating to say it.

"Try living with them." Digby said.

Digby told me he was anxious to start working on a new investigation so he could take a trip overseas to interview potential witnesses. There was something a little desperate in Digby's tone. I realized how disappointed he was about the Horvat case. I felt it too. We had worked hard for the trial and it was disheartening to see it fail, but I think Digby took it harder than most. He always talked about that case and how excited he was the first day when he and Goreman wore their barrister's robes and Digby got to carry the briefcases as they went into the courtroom. Now he was back at square one, he said. I think he just wanted something, *anything*, to happen in his life, other than an expanded waistline.

Digby and I, like the other lawyers and historians, were regularly assigned files to investigate. Goreman sent lists around from time to time as suspects were added and others unaccountably and inconveniently died. Some files held more promise than others, so we tended to focus on those, knowing the others were likely to remain dormant. In my years at the SPU I had completed a tremendous amount of historical research overseas, spending weeks in archives and document centres in Germany, Russia, Poland, and Ukraine. These dusty, cavernous old places could be treasure troves; you simply had to know where to look. The Nazis were fastidious about keeping records and sometimes not fast enough in destroying them, so there were tremendous mounds of material to be perused. I'd make copies of anything that seemed even remotely relevant and then I would bundle up the lot into cardboard boxes and fly back to Canada and try to make some sense of it all.

Much of this material consisted of files and trial records arising from any number of prosecutions conducted by the Soviets and the West Germans. My task was to comb through the endless pages, some simply fragments or scraps, relying on my flimsy German and on the help of the Russian translators in the office. I'd pick out the names of potential witnesses and try to cross-reference other investigations. This might mean more trips overseas, other archives, other document centres. The methodology was of the needle-in-the-haystack sort, at times, but there was really no other way that it could be done.

In February 1993, while Digby was slumming with the Swiss, I'd been poring over a number of KGB investigation files concerning an SS officer named Heinrich Bock. Bock had been implicated in a series of mass executions in and around Kiev in 1941-42. In the 1950s and early 1960s the KGB and the West Germans both conducted investigations, but Bock had never been located. That was not surprising, since by then Bock was residing in Kitchener, Ontario, under the name Henry Birkland. His new name and address in Canada were published in a Soviet newspaper in 1986 in an article condemning Western nations as havens for Nazi killers and being generally decadent and therefore bad. (By 1993 their tune had changed: now they really loved us, and our hard currency.) Bock and several others were named in the article. A copy was sent from the Canadian embassy in Moscow back to Canada. It travelled along a circuitous route that saw it sit in many in-trays and in just as many out-trays. It was handled and folded and marked and highlighted; it was stamped and clipped to memos and then unclipped, and then stapled and then unstapled and passed along again. Finally, it was laid to rest, after a suitable moment of silence, in a manila pocket attached to the Bock (a.k.a. Birkland) file.

I now had dozens of names entered into the Bock database that had cropped up in some fashion in the Soviet and West German files. Some of these people had provided statements or had been interrogated or had simply been mentioned by someone else. It was like a primordial soup, full of fragments, truths, lies, understatements, exaggerations, hunches, lost memories, and solid leads. On Digby's return, he and I commenced the next phase of the Bock investigation.

Now would begin the making of THE LIST.

Digby loved lists. He loved the certainty of them, the confidence with which each name was set out in a column with a summary beside it detailing dates and places of birth, occupations during the war, and a list of statements, if any, provided in any previous investigations. The list for Bock was particularly impressive. There were many names with summaries attached, summaries that were concise, yet comprehensive, compelling, and persuasive. The list contained one hundred and twenty names. Most were Russian or German by birth. Where possible, a last known address was included. When Digby laid eyes on the list his face brightened, as if the memory of two weeks with the smelly Swiss parasites had vanished. In that moment of joy, I could have sworn two pounds of flab fell from his belly and fled out the door.

"This is tremendous!" he said. "I feel like running out and arresting the guy right now. We've got some pretty damning stuff here."

"Yeah, except we still have to find out if any of these people are alive. Some of them would be pretty old now, assuming they survived the war and the KGB."

"Okay, okay, you're right. But a lot of them could still be alive." He pointed to one name on the list. Saliva had seemed to form in the corner of his mouth. "Look at this Probst fellow. He says he saw Bock shooting people in the head. That's great stuff."

"Actually, I think the Soviets might have executed Probst, but it's not clear from their report. I included his name so we can submit it to the Russians and see if he's alive. Maybe he's in Kostroma or Alma Ata."

"Damn Russians," Digby said. "They never want to leave us a thing. Okay, well, we have to work with what we've got. I'll prepare a letter to send to the Germans and the Russians. We can send it today."

This was where it became difficult. Digby deserved my patience, he was an exception of sorts. In the bland, dim hallways and cubbyholes of the SPU, a slight odour was now barely discernible, like the first whiff of chlorine gas drifting past St. Julien and towards the Ypres Salient. Its presence grew day by day. Some sensed it, smelled it, and were gone. A couple of lawyers had already jumped ship, and others might follow. We knew that soon, like those poor bastards at Ypres, we all might have to piss on our handkerchiefs. Digby would stand to the last, and his dedication and interest had to be nurtured, but it also had to be controlled.

"We can't just submit all one hundred and twenty names, Digby. The Germans and the Russians will go nuts and tell us to piss up a rope. They won't try to locate that many people. We have to be realistic, cut some of the names out and make it manageable."

Digby sighed but nodded in agreement. "Okay," he said, "let's do it." He spoke as if I were a surgeon who'd told him the leg would have to come off, and we were out of anesthetic.

We retired to Digby's office and set to work while framed and labelled photographs of Bryndyce – thin smile, nasty little eyes – looked down upon us in judgement. In one photo she was riding a horse in the Loire Valley, in another posing in Provence, or hiking with more Euro-trash in von Trapp–land. She retained a singular facial expression that suggested she was merely indulging the rest of the world. Meanwhile I tried to indulge Digby as we plodded through the list of names. Whenever I suggested a certain name be cut, Digby would sigh and hesitate, as if being asked to part with an old and dear friend.

"Look," I said, "anyone born before 1910 should be cut. They're likely dead and, if alive, they're not likely to be much use."

That led to a protracted discussion of how spry and sharp some people in their eighties or nineties *could* be. Digby said his great-uncle, for example, was one hundred years old and could remember . . . Everyone seems to have some relative who smoked four packs a day and drank like a fish and lived to one hundred and twenty and never forgot a damn thing, except how to die. Life should be so sweet; it wasn't.

"Digby," I said, "it's 1993. Do the math and divide the figure with the simple fact of human biology." My tone was now a little strained. Eventually we arrived at a compromise and decreed that life for our potential witnesses began no sooner than 1908.

Even with that draconian stroke the list was still lengthy and untenable. It was clear from the statements of some of these persons that they had no idea who Bock was, and would not likely have been in a position to provide any information about our suspect. When I suggested that those people could also be cut, Digby began to pick at his scalp and dig away at his hair. That head of hair had commenced the inevitable journey upwards, and the sharp extra-starched creases of his blazer began to lose their definition and soften into scruffiness.

"Maybe they just weren't asked about Bock."

"In most cases I think we can safely assume if they knew anything about Bock they would have said so."

"But if they weren't specifically asked, and maybe if your summaries are too general . . . ?"

He knew he was treading into dangerous waters and could see my mounting frustration. *Christ!*

To resolve these disputes, we dug out the actual statements from the document room and Digby pored over the questions and answers. Some of these interrogations, especially those led by the KGB, had been conducted over several days, so the process of reading them was a lengthy one. I felt there was no point telling Digby that any KGB statement had to be taken with a large grain of salt. If the Soviets didn't like what a witness/suspect had to say, they might put a bullet in the base of his skull and finish off the statement without him. Sometimes the truth was just about winners and losers.

It took two days of haggling until a list was hashed out. Digby looked exhausted and a little distressed by the process, like the platoon leader who'd had to leave half his boys on that stretch of beach. I was simply relieved. The final list contained sixty names, which Digby sent to the Germans, the Russians, and the Ukrainians, with a letter attached above Goreman's signature. Three months later the Germans sent their reply. Another month after that we heard from the Russians, and then the Ukrainians. All told, twenty persons were located; four were living in Kiev, and sixteen were spread out in various locations in eastern Ukraine. Everyone else was dead, missing, or simply unknown. Digby's face fell, and he wondered if we should have submitted more names. I said we were lucky to find twenty, and left it at that.

He and Viaux would conduct the interviews. They arranged to travel at the end of June. Meanwhile, I moved on to another file, working on yet another list, feeling the ghosts rise from the pages of each document as I scoured them for names.

IV

On June 22, 1993, Digby and Viaux left for Kiev and Elizabeth Brunswick first set foot in my office. I remember the date exactly. It was the same date the Germans had invaded Russia in 1941, which meant that her arrival wasn't necessarily a good thing, but was nonetheless noteworthy in my mind. It was the day that I fell in love with her, though I didn't know it at the time. It's hard to be precise about those sorts of things. It's like saying that this was the day I inhaled the germ that gave me that nasty cold. I didn't realize it, yet nevertheless it happened.

I received no warning of her arrival; no memorandum had been circulated, no announcement made. She just appeared, and I first saw her when she knocked on my open door that morning. I looked up from a pile of papers like some sort of scruffy weasel peering up from its den. I saw a tall, slim woman, with curly dark hair tied at the back, staring at me with blue eyes that were lidded in a way that made her look rather reserved. She wore a black skirt and a black blazer, buttoned up, still revealing a triangle of white flesh below the nape of her neck.

"Elizabeth Brunswick," she said, and she extended a hand. *A polite smile, eyes a little cold.* I took her hand in mine.

Her fingers were long and thin and her hand felt quite soft. She said she was starting here today but there'd been no one to meet her. I was the first person she'd seen. There was a trace of irritation in her voice, and something else too – a touch of bitterness perhaps. I'm not the most discerning fellow in the world, but even I could tell that this was not a happy woman.

"Actually, a lot of people are away at the moment. You know, overseas, interview trips, that sort of thing, and I think the boss is at some war-crimes conference in The Hague, or something."

"Graham Goreman?"

"Gone till next week. Anyway, have a seat, I'll give you the tour in a moment."

She sat down. *Black sheer stockings, rising up slim, smooth calves.* The scent of her wafted towards me, subtle, expensive, citrus and spice. It was the scent that first clutched me. No one else, nothing else at this place, ever smelled like that. I was surprised that the whole building didn't shut down, invaded now by something, *someone*, who didn't reek of the bland or the dusty or the stale.

She told me that she was from Toronto, a prosecutor with the Prosecution Service, which at first she called the AG, as if I should have known that brand of slang. She said she wasn't here for good, though; she made that abundantly clear. It would be a nine-month secondment. As she put it, "That was the deal." She said this with great emphasis, as if hoping it had not been forgotten. Then she'd get to return to Toronto, where she belonged. There was an edge to her tone.

"No offence, but why did you come here?" I asked.

"No offence taken." She smoothed the fabric of her skirt that lay softly on her lap, accentuating those gentle folds. Her lap did not need smoothing. "I'm serving a conditional sentence. If I behave I'll be paroled and maybe earn an early release."

I took this to be more of that brand of AG slang. Whatever she meant, I could tell that she was not pleased with her life, but her tone suggested I would not be her confidant, not now anyway.

"Well, let me give you the tour." My enthusiasm was not well received, but she did thank me.

We did the rounds, though it did not take long. The place seemed almost vacant, and I could see she was not impressed. It's not that people weren't busy, or that the work was not being done. As I had informed her, most people were off doing research or interviewing witnesses in a desperate bid to recover the initiative and bring another man, any man, into court.

At the end of the little tour, we stood in front of my office for a moment. There was a moment of silence as I struggled to think of something to say. By nature I am horrified of small talk. I think of the interminable airplane journeys, bus trips, and elevator rides of my past where I've been trapped with gregarious commuters, impervious to my indifference, blathering on about the weather, the airworthiness of an aircraft, the mechanical acuity of cables and pulleys, or the health of some local sports franchise that I could not care less about. Give me silence any day, but not today, not when I needed a phrase or a sentence or some witty remark that might make her stay. But nothing sprang to mind.

"So, uh, welcome aboard."

Fuck.

I believe a trace of a tear appeared in one of her eyes, so delighted was she that fate had sent her to this neck of the woods. Then she turned and walked down the hall, still elegant and graceful, though in full retreat.

So much for the welcome wagon.

For the rest of that week, since there were some journals and secondary sources I had to review, I worked at the Faculty of History at the University of Ottawa, my old haunt. I obtained my master's here three years before at the same time as I was working at the SPU, and the smell of the study halls and the library brought back memories of late nights and bad coffee, fast-food dinners and endless battles with the Beast, my dissertation on the rise of National Socialism in Germany. I did prevail and the Beast was tamed. And yet I thought I caught a glimpse of him, of It, near a study carrel, much diminished in size and peeking around a stack of dusty volumes: discarded piles of Foucault, "Martyrs of pies, and reliques of the bum."

I looked closer and the creature was gone, a shadow that vanished. Relieved, my past now behind me, I left the library and walked back through the campus, over the canal bridge, and back to the SPU. It was Friday and after five, which meant that the downtown of the city would be practically abandoned, like that town in *The Andromeda Strain*. Indeed it was, and after I dropped off my notes in my office I began to walk home, solitary, on empty sidewalks.

As I walked along Queen Street I heard the rapping, the tap-tap-tapping on the thick glass of the big window of the bar. It was Elizabeth. She waved at me to come in. I knew the place, or I had known it in its previous incarnation. It had once been called the Crusty Barnacle. That was more than four years ago now. Then it had been a dingy place: dumpy, smelly, and none too clean, as if everything in it was covered in a glaze, the beery surfaces of each pint of ale or bitter covered with a film. I liked the place, though, and I'd meet my friends from university there from time to time. Even Viaux and I went there sometimes in that first year we worked at the SPU.

The last time I had gone there was with my girlfriend at the time. That was almost three years ago. We met there after work. I ordered a pint, asked her about her day, and she told me she was leaving me for an architect named Jake. There was no debate. In her eyes at that moment I could see I was gone from her life. She tried to say it was because we wanted different things, we were growing apart, *blah, blah, blah*. I think she'd been reading some of that spew from the Personal Growth sections of her numerous magazines in preparation for the break-up. For her it had to be *about something*, as if our break-up and our relationship were something profound, so deep in meaning that it had to be labelled and explained, with watery platitudes and feel-good truisms, like the kind you read in greeting cards or on posters with puppies or flowers: all dreck.

It was all rather simple, I thought. First we were strangers, we met, we kissed, we fucked, we could not live apart for one second, then we got bored, and then we moved on and became strangers again. No grand design, no scheme. We're solitary blobs of flesh, and nerve endings and sparking brains that bounce around colliding into one another before career-ing off somewhere else. Put that in a greeting card.

I was hurt, of course, and wondered for a while if she'd change her mind and maybe call. She never did, because no one ever does. I thought about her and Jake, imagining him to be some blue-eyed, blondish chappie, raffish and rich, with friends nicknamed Deeker or the Kegmeister and a hefty trust fund. I was wrong, of course. I saw them together a few months later, near the walkway along the canal. It was the fall and very sunny. We chatted for what seemed about forty seconds, though it was probably a bit longer than that. He looked mortified and quite uncomfortable and I noticed with delight that I was taller and better-looking. She looked heavier too, made plump, I suppose, with self-satisfied content, thinking, no doubt, that I still missed her. She had a perm now, with tight curls, and wore an outfit I'd never seen before, a kind of sporty denim and cotton look, her collar up. It didn't suit her. He looked a bit like Adolf Eichmann, except younger, and with glasses and a little more hair, and, well, not so evil either, just kind of small and nervous. His bluejeans were very neat and looked as if they'd been ironed. He struck me as being one of those fastidious guys who loved systems and plans and ejaculated over e-mails and com-puter gadgetry, and always vacuumed out their cars.

I was relieved to bid them farewell, but I was sad for a while. She was different now, a stranger. I hadn't changed, though. After that I spent more time at work, and I never went back to the Barnacle. It was a dump anyway.

Now it was apparently known as Ye Olde Jolly Roger, a franchise, brimming with Brit-kitsch: Toby jugs, banners for

Manchester United, coats of arms, and all sorts of Celtic shit on the walls. It was perfect for the denizens of Langley Manors and Cotswold Estates. Needless to say, the place was packed. It smelled of smoke and beer. I walked around the bar to the booth where Elizabeth was seated. She was alone, but there were two pint glasses on the table.

"I'm on a date," she said, betraying nothing in the way of enthusiasm or joy.

"Oh, well, then I'll let you . . ."

"No, no, please stay, Dennis." She said this with a trace of panic. "It's a very bad date. He's throwing up in the men's room, I'm sorry, *the loo*." She was dressed elegantly and her hair was different now, cut short, accentuating her long neck. It was apparent that her evening was not going well. "Oh, here we go," she said. "My escort for the evening has returned. This is Rick." She rolled her eyes when she said this.

Rick was in his early thirties. His was a prep-school look, I suppose: suit, tie, lantern jaw. The whole deal. One problem, though. Rick's complexion was mottled with shocking shades of white and green. Truly, white and green. This, combined with his almost falling down into and *under* the booth, foamy splashes of yellow vomit on his suit, and his inability to talk, led to the inexorable conclusion that Rick was shitfaced and down for the count.

I was going to sit beside Rick, but I was a bit wary, given his appearance. My guess was that Rick had a bit more purging to endure and I did not want to be in the line of fire. I perched on Elizabeth's side of the booth, not wanting to sit too close to her either. I'm not sure why. She didn't seem to

notice, and lit a cigarette as we both watched Rick's efforts
to keep his head and his body in an upright position, no
mean feat. She stared at him with a look of black hate and
drew heavily on her cigarette. Rick was silent, his mouth
opening and shutting like a fish's, his eyes moving independent of one another, unfocused, uncomprehending.

"You see, Dennis," Elizabeth said, still staring at her beau,
"Richard, or *Rick*, was so thrilled about our date this evening
that he spent the afternoon here, with his buddies, all big
movers and shakers in the world of corporate law, *don't you
know*, drinking shooters and pineapple martinis, since, I
would guess, about lunchtime."

Rick sprang into action at that moment and scrambled
back out of the booth and towards the gents. I safely assumed
that a session of projectile vomiting shortly ensued.
Meanwhile, a jukebox was playing "Come On Eileen."

Elizabeth butted out her cigarette, slamming its glowing
end into the ashtray, crushing it into submission. She began
to slide herself out of the booth. "It would appear that
dinner at La Nuit is off," she said.

Then she looked at me. "Do you want to go somewhere?
Seriously, let's go. I just want to get out of this horrible place.
If you have other plans, I'll understand." I appreciated that
she had given me the benefit of the doubt on the question of
Friday-night plans.

"No, no," I said. "There's a pub on Elgin that's not too
bad. Not like this anyway. What about Rick?"

"He can get the tab."

It was hot and very humid, and Elgin Street was quite busy, unlike the wasteland of centre-town a few blocks away. As we walked I could smell her perfume again. She was wearing a short dark-blue skirt and a loose linen blazer. She was quiet as we walked and I wondered if perhaps she was shy or simply bored. We reached Elgin Street, and the bar, where we sat outside on the terrace. While we waited for a litre of wine, we watched the people walk to and fro. Cars honked at some jaywalkers. A couple of Harleys roared by.

"You've cut your hair," I said.

She tugged at it a little and ran her hand through it. "It's too short," she said, and pulled at it again as if to make it grow back immediately.

"I like it," I said, not trying to sound too interested. "You've got very nice hair."

She looked at me, and thanked me as the wine arrived.

"I wonder how Rick is doing?" I said. This made her laugh, and even in the fading light her face brightened.

"He'll survive." She reached into her purse and brought out her pack of cigarettes.

"Boyfriend?" I asked.

"No, thank God. We once dated in Toronto, off and on. He called me two nights ago and said he would be in Ottawa this week, appearing in the *Supreme Court*." She deepened the tone of her voice as she said this, imitating a boastful, pompous Rick. "He proposed drinks, dinner at a nice place, and no doubt hoped to be hopping into my bed around midnight."

"I think he's out of luck."

"He's a jerk anyway, and full of crap. I only said yes to

him because I was lonely and bored. Do you know Rick wasn't even arguing in court this morning? He was there on a watching brief."

"Which means?"

"His firm represents some third party that has an interest in the results of this appeal heard in the Supreme Court today. Rick was sent there just to sit in the audience and watch the proceedings. He didn't even have to take notes, but he made it sound as if he was leading the charge, battling it out with the highest court in the land. You know, I'm so sick of lawyers these days. Full of themselves. Pompous, tedious idiots. It's not a profession any more, it's a trade, like selling shoes. For every true talent, every real litigator, there are about fifty Ricks, mouthy, lying moral relativists, bottom-feeders, and whores, the lot of them."

Her eyes narrowed as she said this, and she appeared angry again.

Such a dark gaze, I thought. Her face was transformed, eyes suddenly black, cold and focused. I said nothing.

"Sorry," she said. "Now I'll just drink wine and become belligerent."

"I understand, you're pissed off. You've had a lousy night so far, a bad date, and I don't imagine you're thrilled about your new work assignment, either."

"You don't miss a trick," she said, the black look again. "You *must* have a master's. Any other brilliant insights you wish to offer?"

She was a very pretty woman, and I was beginning to think she was rather charming, but she turned on me in a flash with that comment and it set me off. I couldn't stand that kind of bile flung my way.

"Just one," I said, as I reached for my wallet and began to rise from the table, all the while trying to remain calm. "For someone who's fresh out of friends, you're rather cocky tonight. You deserve yourself. Rick got off easy. Have a nice night."

She sat up very quickly with a look of alarm. Her hand shot out towards me. "Wait, I'm sorry. You're right, I'm being odious. I didn't mean to insult you. I'm just really on edge. Stay and finish your drink." She sighed and said, "White flag?"

"Okay," I said, "white flag." I reluctantly sat down.

"Two people with tempers."

She drained her glass and I poured her some more wine. I filled my own glass, too, and I felt a little sheepish, as if I'd overreacted.

She took a little breath. "So where were you going tonight, walking past the bar? Subject change, small talk." She was grinning. "I'm trying to be charming now."

"Okay. I was going home, not too far from here. I rent the top floor of a house on Meltcalfe, up Elgin a ways and around the corner."

"Nice?"

"It's a *heritage home.*" I pronounced the words with a mock-patrician tone. "Translation: it's too small and the rent is far too high. I'd almost feel better if my landlord showed up the first of each month wearing a balaclava and shoved a pistol into my face; instead of clearing out my till, I write him postdated cheques. But, it's close to the office, no long bus rides, no need for a car."

"I've found an apartment hotel," she said. "Translation: it's fairly large, empty, ugly, charmless, and temporary, and of course *free*. My office in Toronto pays. Afterwards I go back to my place in the Annex."

"So why are you here? What happened?"

"I made a mistake," she said, flicking her tongue very sharply across her upper lip. "I made a stupid mistake." She shook her head with impatience. "It was just some crap at work. I'll do my penance and atone for my sins and make the most of my exile. Then it'll be old news." She seemed to be trying to convince herself. "Why aren't you on a date or something?"

I noticed how she'd do that a lot, switch topics in the blink of an eye, as if she didn't want to dwell on any one thing for too long, especially anything about herself.

I shrugged. "I don't have a girl at the moment. Self-imposed exile. I had a girlfriend and now I don't. I'm quite used to being by myself, and quite content."

She smiled rather coldly.

"Are you from here?" she asked, narrowing her eyes, seeming to study me.

"No, but I hardly go back to Winnipeg now. I have little connection to the place. My friends have moved on, I've moved on. Very simple. My mother still lives there, though. I go home at Christmas and Easter. Short visits are all I can endure."

She laughed. "I like the way your sentences get shorter

and shorter the more you talk about yourself. You're turning into a clam."

"For good reason. What about you?"

"Okay. Family: parents dead, sister estranged. Status: married once, two years ago, lasted four months. Reason: I was an idiot, husband a narcissistic creep, loved himself more than he did me, left with an aerobics instructor named Kerri. Quick divorce. Two tawdry, brief affairs follow in rapid succession, rapidly terminated. I don't include Rick."

"Nicely put," I said, trying to look impressed by her brevity. The litre of wine was now empty and our server, an uninterested Gen-X prat, in a moment of absent-mindedness was actually offering to serve us. I looked at Elizabeth and she nodded in agreement. I ordered another litre of white.

It was simple, really. Neither of us had any other place to go.

Another envelope arrived this morning. I read from the pages
enclosed within.

Excerpt from Report of Unterstürmführer Dr. Becker

May 16, 1942

"I ordered the vans of Einsatzgruppe D to be
camouflaged as house trailers by putting one set of
windows on each side of the small van and two on each
side of the larger vans. Even with such disguise I must
report that the vans quickly became well known to the
civilian population, who nicknamed the vehicles soul-
destroyers [*Seelenvernichter*] and would call out and point
as soon as one of them appeared. It is obvious, in my
opinion, that despite efforts to the contrary the vans
cannot be kept secret for any length of time, not even
camouflaged.

"I should like to take this opportunity to bring the
following to your attention: several kommandos have
had the unloading after the application done by their
own men. I brought to the attention of the commander

of those kommandos concerned the immense psychological injuries and damages to their health which that work can have for those men, even if not immediately, at least later on.

"The application of gas is usually not undertaken correctly. In order to come to an end as fast as possible, the driver presses the accelerator to the fullest extent. By doing that the persons to be executed suffer death from suffocation and not death by dozing off as originally planned. My directions now have proved that by correct adjustment of the levers death comes faster and the prisoners fall asleep peacefully. Distorted faces and excretions, as could be seen before, are no longer noticed. . . ."

That night I dreamed of Richmaier the interpreter. It was spring and the sun was warm. I stood in the garden behind my stone house in Winnipeg. I saw him working with a shovel, digging up the wet black soil. Clumps clung to the sharp edges of the shovel. He waved at me as I approached, as if greeting a long-lost friend. His black uniform, its lapels adorned with white diamonds and SS runes, was now in tatters. His eyes were wide and dark, troubled, his lips colourless. He looked as he did that time we spoke in the mess hall in Taganrog. That was when he told me about the Russian prisoners left to perish at a railway siding. "Do you know that they are all still here? The corpses, I mean. They are all still here, Friedrich. Just where we left them. I can do nothing about it, your garden is full of them, so many bodies, like that time at Mariupol. . . .

Once Baumer screamed at me, that time when I vomited, when we first used the gas van, black trucks with the windows painted on the sides so we could fool people and make them look safe. *Dushegubka*. The soul-destroyers, the black ravens. That was what the Russians called them. The trucks were still new then and they didn't work as well as the ones that followed. . . . Do you remember their faces? Those large, bulging eyes, sightless, benign, like shiny marble, and horrible, black pupils like tiny dots. That was the very last part of them that was human. That was where the life of them had been quenched, in the eyes, those black, empty, and shiny eyes . . . and the shit and the urine . . . because they had died so slow and not in the way that had been expected. It was not efficient . . . such slow deaths were not efficient and that had to be remedied. Improvements had to be made. The *aktionen* had to be kept secret. . . . We were ordered to hide the bodies. And what did we do? We dug deeper holes but we never dug deep enough. You see?" He pointed down to his feet where part of an arm and a leg and another arm and other legs had begun to emerge from the soil. The flesh was white, with green and blue hues. "We should have made the holes deeper. Then no one would have known."

He told me that the Russians had caught him because he had stayed behind at Novorossijsk. "They killed me. I told them the Germans forced me to do these things, and Fedorov and his company of HiWis. They were the ones who should have been punished. I said that they were the ones who did those things, but they didn't believe me. They shot me in the head. I was sentenced to hang, like Fedorov and Psarev and the others who were caught. But when I walked down a corridor to my cell someone came up from behind. I felt the pressure of a cold steel cylinder and then the burst of heat. It was just as well. I told you that I should not have seen those things.

He told me, "They'll come for you. One day . . . they'll come for you." He had begun to cry and, looking down at the patch of soil, he said, "Your garden is ruined." Then he handed me the shovel and I saw how his hands and boots were covered with black mud. He walked away from me and, though I called out to him, he kept walking until he vanished. "I never wanted this," he said.

In the spring of 1943 we were sent to Mozyr to fight partisans in the Pripet Marshes. It was a *Grossaktion* with the whole of the kommando involved. We were based in a village called Shuki, a primitive-looking place: houses made of wood with thatched roofs, wretched and melancholy; huts made of sod, like caves sitting above the ground. Attached to every house was a pen for livestock. The people were mostly peasants who wore quilted coats with thick belts and white peaked caps. The land around us was featureless, flat, low, full of marshes and thick forests, a horrid country.

We scoured the villages and forests for partisans and Jews, burning every village to the ground, leaving no traces. We understood our orders and our objectives. We heard that the news from the Eastern Front was bad. The Russians were moving westward without cease, and any day now the British and the Americans would invade in the west. And yet we carried on. Christmann drove us on, and we obeyed. We were a plague that spread quickly, deadly and thorough.

The last *Aktion* I remember was near Kostiukowichi in a small village beside a collection of trees. There were several wells there. Three days before, two kommando men had been ambushed and killed near the village by partisans, and Christmann ordered a punitive raid. In the early morning, when the sun had begun to rise, we descended upon that village and rousted the inhabitants. There were four wells in the village, dry pits now, but they would do. I felt nothing, absolutely nothing. That is how I remember it now, it was as if I was filled with dust. I was tired, too, like the other men. We wanted to do the job quickly and get out, move on. The war was going badly for Germany. I had no illusions now. This was all a matter of time now.

At the village the people were herded towards the wells. I cannot say now if there were children, but I remember old men, and women. At the time it did not matter to me; I simply acted and saw nothing. We shot them. I took my turn with the rest. When we fired, the bodies fell into the wells. Afterwards the village was burned and we moved on. We left nothing behind.

In the fall of 1943, the kommando was disbanded and I was sent to Könitz, in East Prussia, to join a new unit known as Squad 41. From there I was sent to Yugoslavia to fight bands of partisans resisting the Germans. Holtzmann and Nachtigal were in the same squad, though I saw little of them because, soon after I arrived, I was wounded by a grenade when our squad was ambushed by partisans. The grenade exploded near my right side, but I was lucky because I was crouched down beside a tree and it absorbed some of the blast. That was a piece of luck. Still, I almost died from loss of blood.

I was sent to a military hospital in Austria, where it took months for me to recover. Because I contracted diphtheria and then typhus while I was there, I was still at the hospital when I learned that the war had ended.

In June 1945 I heard rumours from some of the other patients. I was told that the British, the Americans, and the Russians had sent intelligence officers out to scour the hospitals, to interrogate some of the patients. There was a new patient in the bed beside me who said these rumours were true. He had been at another hospital and had seen some SS men being taken away. His name, I remember, was Veikh.

One morning, we sat outside in the sun on wooden chairs set upon a terrace behind the hospital. I was still quite weak and it was very pleasant to sit outside; the warm sun felt rejuvenating. I could see the Alps in the distance, many kilometres away. There were other wounded patients on the terrace, some with shattered limbs, some blind, some with no faces, some no longer resembling human beings.

Veikh sat beside me on the terrace. He said he was an SS grenadier, a warrant officer who'd seen active service in Russia and Normandy. Part of his face had been destroyed by a Russian shell. One-eyed, he could still form a grin with his lips, but the effect was ghastly. One side of his face was seared, as if he wore a mask of scarred flesh. The eye socket and cheekbone on the right side were shattered and part of his nose had been cut away.

"I saw the British take a group of Waffen-SS officers away with them from the last hospital I was at," he said. "They missed me, though. Perhaps they thought I was as good as dead."

"What were they looking for?" I asked, trying not to betray any interest. He was not fooled, I'm sure. He knew I was worried about the Russians.

"Very simple," he said. He lifted his arm and pointed to the spot underneath. It was a blood-grouping tattoo. He said all the SS men had them.

"They look for this. This is the mark of Cain, I think. I once saw a man at the hospital carving away at his own flesh to slice it off. But that's no good. The scar gives you away. They'll know. Even if you cut your arm off, they'll know."

"What do they want?" I asked him.

"They're the victors and they want to punish the losers. That's what it's all about. We would have done the same, I think. They want revenge. It just depends who wins and who loses. But why are you worried? You don't look like SS. They won't care about you. Where did you serve, Reile?"

"I was an interpreter in Krasnodar and Rostov. Other places, too."

"SD?" He asked. His one eye narrowed as he looked at me. "Sicherheitsdienst?"

"Yes," I said. *He knew then.* My eyes widened as I tried to explain. "But I was simply an interpreter. I don't think that they will be interested in me."

"SD. An interpreter with the SD." He mulled this over for a bit and nodded very slowly as my information sunk in. "I think it will be bad for you then, Reile. The Russians will be interested in you after all. You're German, *ja*? *Volksdeutscher*, I know, but still German. That's good enough for the Ivans. Ukraine, Russia, you were there, *ja*? So was I, Reile. I know about what happened. I remember. One doesn't forget these things. We were ordered to keep quiet: no pictures, no letters, but we all know what was done, what we had to do. The Russians may have taken my face from me but I still have my memories." He began to recite words that I recognized. "*Tötungseinsätze . . . Judenaktionen . . . Erschiessungeinsätze . . . Judenerschiessungen . . .* So many names for the same thing."

"It was a dirty business," I said, hastily. "I simply obeyed orders, like you." I remember what Zeetzen said when he addressed the kommando at Mariupol. He told us we had to rely upon our inner toughness to perform these tasks.

Veikh grinned. It was not the face of a human being, but his one eye still hinted of life and intelligence. It was his eye that prevailed, peering from behind that mask. That was all that seemed to be left of him, that and his crooked smile.

"So you think we are one and the same then, young Reile?" His tone was sharper now.

I had offended him.

"I simply meant . . ."

"I know what you meant. Yes, we all have shit on our hands. I obeyed orders, perhaps not always the same ones you obeyed . . ." His voice trailed off. Then he calmed himself and began to speak again. "I remember the bits and pieces of what happened," he said. "In September 1941, after Barbarossa, when we were still invincible, we rolled across the great steppes, the endless fields of wheat, the plains that stretched forever. We moved so fast then and there were so many

prisoners. My platoon was resting at a place near the Dnieper
River in the Christoforowka region. We were lying down in
the grass, dirty, thirsty, tired. It was quite hot too, I remember."

At that moment he paused as we watched a patient, a
young man, who was wheeled past us in a chair by a nurse.
He was without legs and arms, and part of his jaw was
missing. The nurse pushed his chair to the edge of the terrace
with the best view of the mountains. She put a blanket
around the boy's shoulders and sat down beside him.

Veikh pointed at the boy. "I may not have a face, but I
have arms and legs and my balls and I can walk. It can
always be worse, eh, Reile? You will always find someone in
a worse predicament than yourself." He chuckled and the
sound of his dry laughter left me chilled. I understood his
meaning. He hoped the Russians would overlook him and
take me first.

"There was an officer," Veikh continued. "I did not know
him, he was SD, some fucking martinet. He appeared that day
in September, when my men were resting, and ordered me
to march my men half a kilometre to a collective farm, some
shithole in Ukraine: dirty villages and towns, cowshit and
mud everywhere, sullen peasants living in wooden huts. I said
to the SD officer, 'Look at my men. We've had no rest for
days. We're good for nothing right now!' But the officer said
that this was an order, a priority. So I obeyed and my men
and I marched along a dirt track that led to a large farm. The
Russians had dug anti-tank trenches before they'd retreated.
You must have seen many such trenches?"

I nodded, not wanting to reveal too much. I did not trust
him now. He talked a lot and I did not like his questions. But

when he asked about the trenches he was not looking at me. He was staring off in the direction of the boy in the wheel-chair and the distant Alps.

I had seen trenches like that. Sometimes the kommando had forced prisoners to dig the trenches deeper and wider so there would be more room to bury the bodies. We should have made the trenches deeper so that the bodies would be hidden for good.

He continued to speak, his eye now on me again. "We entered the perimeter of the collective farm. We saw three wells but they were almost all dried up. We weren't there to collect water, though. The SD officer arrived in a small car. He said that the Jews had already been rounded up and were secured in two huge barns. I never saw the Jews, I just heard them in barns, cries, screams. An Einsatzkommando was deployed there around two of the wells. The officer told us to open up the barns and herd the Jews towards the wells. We opened the first barn and stood on the perimeter and the SD men went to work. They called it a *Brunnen-aktion*, a well operation. They put those dried-up wells to good use. They filled them up, and then they used the anti-tank trenches the Russians had dug around the farm. You must have seen those things?"

I said that this was how it was usually done. I felt sick inside as he spoke.

"There was a problem, though. Nothing ever goes quite to plan. My men couldn't open the door of that second barn. We struggled with it and I said, 'Enough,' and I ordered my men to fire their machine guns into that barn through the walls and two small windows. Then we torched the barn and the flames took care of the rest. The barn burned to ash. The SD officer was furious. He said, 'How can I make a proper count for my reports? How can I provide an accurate tally?' I thought about shooting him, too. I would have shoved a grenade right up his ass, but it was not worth it. My men and I went back to fighting the Russians after that." He cackled a little and I wondered if he was insane. It frightened me to hear him speak. He wanted me to know that he was no worse than I.

I inquired again about the Russians. "Will they try to take me away?" I asked, hoping he might somehow reassure me. I did not want to think about what they might do to me.

"The Russians?" he said. "Yes, I expect the Russians will want to speak to you, and then they will shoot you. But think, Reile, even if we had won the war, you'd have to go back to the east to finish the job you'd started."

The next day the grenadier was moved to another ward. I never saw him again.

When I recovered from my wounds and my illnesses I was taken away, but not by the Russians. By some good fortune I was rounded up with a group of others at the hospital and transported by the British to another prisoner-of-war camp farther west, in Austria. I heard there were camps everywhere now, full of Germans, Rumanians, Ukrainians, and Cossacks. I heard too that there were special camps for the Waffen-SS, but I was put in a camp full of soldiers, Wehrmacht. We were hungry all the time, and cold, too. At that camp I waited and I barely spoke to anyone, and never about the kommando.

Three months later, in December 1945, I was taken out of the camp in a British transport truck to a compound a few kilometres away. I feared for my life as I sat in the transport, but I was relieved to a degree when I saw that I had arrived at a British camp. By now I could recognize their uniforms and vehicles. I was taken out of the transport by two British soldiers who had sat in the transport with me during the journey, chatting with one another and eyeing me periodically.

They took me to a sort of hut with wooden sides, a wooden door, and a canvas roof. Inside the hut, another soldier told me to sit on a chair placed in the middle of the hut in front of a table. I was left alone for several minutes. I thought of what the SS grenadier had told me. I thought of Mariupol and Taganrog and the pits, the balka. My mind was racing now. I wondered what the British knew. I knew the Russians weren't far from here, a short drive perhaps. That thought terrified me. I tried to think of what the British might want to know, but my mind was blank. I did not know what I should say. I kept thinking of the SS grenadier's eye and his horrible, dry cackling.

Then an officer came into the hut, a captain or a major perhaps. He was thin, slight, with sharp features and a thick, pressed khaki uniform. He wore spectacles and carried a sort of folder underneath one arm. When I heard him enter I stood to attention, but he told me right away to sit down. He spoke to me in German in a manner that was very clipped and impatient. I watched him place the folder on the table. It was full of papers that he began to remove and place on the table beside the folder.

He began by reading out my name and date of birth and asking me if both were correct. I said that they were. Then he pulled out a folded set of documents from the file. I could see that a photograph was attached to one of the pages. He told me that these were copies of my citizenship records and my record of military service. His eyes then focused upon me. Through his spectacles I saw eyes that were severe, blue like ice and unwavering. I felt them drill through me and I had to look away. I felt weak, nervous.

He began to fire questions at me in a loud voice that cut through the close air in the hut.

"You became a German citizen in May 1944?"

"Yes, sir."

"How?"

"I was permitted to apply by my commanding officer because I was an ethnic German."

"And because you served with an SS unit, correct?"

"I was never with the SS, sir, I was an interpreter. I simply translated orders for the German police and sometimes for Wehrmacht officers when they were dealing with the local populace or collaborating units."

"You're lying." I felt my cheeks burn and my heart race. "Your *Eiwanderungszentrale* card states that you are a member of the SD and the Security Police with a rank of SS-*Mann* at the time you obtained your German citizenship. That means you are a member of the SS, doesn't it?"

His lips were thin and pale and he formed them into a little smile. He knew that he had me.

"The papers must be mistaken, sir." My voice was frail now, almost a whisper.

He stood up and walked towards me and flung some of the papers full into my face. They fell across my chest and onto the floor at my feet.

"You're a liar. Those are your papers, Reile. There's no mistake about that. Pick them up. Look at them. Look at the photographs. That's you. That's your name, that's your face. That's your EWZ card, is it not?" He stood close to me, yelling into my ear.

I picked up the documents and looked at them. My hands shook and a bead of sweat dropped from my forehead onto one of the papers. The officer was still smiling.

"Yes," I said, "those are my documents, but I was never a member of the SS . . ."

"Put the papers on the table."

I did as he ordered. My hands still shook and I cursed myself for not being able to disguise my fear. The officer watched me for a moment. Then he sat down on the edge of the desk a foot or two from where I sat. He spoke and his voice was much softer.

"You are a young man, Reile. You could survive. It's up to me, you know. I have the authority to let you live. It's me that decides if you can stay in Germany and move on with your life, move past all of this. Don't be foolish, and don't take me for a fool. You have one more chance." He gestured with his head towards the door of the hut. "Do you know what lies a few yards from here, out that door?"

I said I did not.

"The Russians. There's a hut near here, not two hundred yards from where you are seated. In that hut there are five Soviet intelligence officers. Right now they're sitting there, with your file. They have a list with your name on it. All it takes is for me to march you over there. That's the difference between life and death now, Reile, two hundred yards. They'll shoot you, of course, but not until they've extracted every piece of information they can possibly get from you. And I dare say they'd be quite interested in the likes of you: ss, sd, Security Police."

He gripped my cheeks and jaw with cold fingers and twisted my face up to face him. He stared down at me with those eyes. "That will be the end of you. You will disappear into a big, black hole." He let go of my face and walked back behind his table and sat down. The hut was silent and he continued to stare at me.

"Perhaps they'll hang you, though, make an example of you. A trial perhaps. Do you wish a trial, Reile?

I did not know if he wished an answer from me.

"There are plenty more where you've come from, you're small potatoes. But I will give you a second chance. You are Friedrich Reile and you were born March 25, 1924, yes?"

"Yes, sir."

"And you were an interpreter serving with an sd unit in southern Russia, correct?"

I hesitated.

He looked at me again. His eyes now revealed an absence of emotion, not hateful, not malicious, not caring. "Two hundred yards," he said.

"I was only an interpreter," I said. "The unit I served with did not have a name or a designation. . . . I wore a uniform but it did not have any markings . . . and I did not hold any kind of rank. . . . I was not a member of the ss. . . . I heard about shootings of partisans and spies and of the Jews but I had no part in any of that . . . I never saw such things. . . . I was just an interpreter. . . ."

He threw up one hand to silence me. He stood over me now.

"You misunderstand me. I know about the Jews and the liquidations, that's not what you're here for. I know that you were in the thick of it, you and your lot. But if I wanted to talk to killers there's plenty others bigger than you. I want to know about your other duties. I want to know about spy networks and intelligence. I want to know about your enemy, Reile, the Soviets, because, you see, they will soon be my enemy, too. Tell me about Krasnodar, Reile, and the NKVD. What did you see? I want names and places and codes if you know them."

My voice was weak now, as soft as a whisper, and tears formed in my eyes, and I knew at that moment that I would tell him everything that I knew. I would tell him what he wanted to hear if it meant that I might stay alive. I told him about the documents I had seen in Krasnodar, the ones the NKVD had left behind. I told him about the numbers of commissars that had been arrested, along with spies and partisans. I told him about the interrogations I witnessed in the cells below our headquarters. I told him any number of details, facts, or figures that I might have heard or read. I remember little of it now, but the officer was very interested. He was quite friendly now. He did not care about the trenches, about the gas vans or the shootings. He wanted to know about Russian spy techniques and networks.

"You see, we're making progress now. I'm going to have

a stenographer brought in to record your statement. Would you like some water?"

I was interrogated by the same officer for several hours over a period of three days. On the third day, the interrogation was complete and I was transported to another prison camp in Germany, where I remained for almost one year. No one like that British officer ever spoke to me again. In December 1946 I was released.

During the war I had regularly written to my mother and sister. In 1943 they had fled to Germany and obtained their citizenship, as did I in 1944. By the time I was released from the last camp my mother had died, so I joined my sister, who now lived in Marburg. She was the only friend I had in this world. She was the only connection that I had to a time before the war and all those other things that followed. We never heard from my father or my brother. They simply disappeared.

My sister met me at the train station when I arrived in Marburg. I had not seen her since before I had been wounded in Yugoslavia, when I had been on leave, but I had been permitted to write to her from the POW camps in Austria. She was one year younger than I. Now she was very pretty, but quite thin. Food was often still scarce. She met me on the platform and kissed me on the cheek and hugged me with such intensity that I thought I might collapse into her arms and weep. I had not felt such softness, such affection, in years. I wanted to hide inside her arms, so that my memories of the war might vanish and I could be innocent again. She held my head and ran her fingers through my hair and told me we would be all right now.

I remained in Marburg. Though it bore some scars from the war, it had for the most part been spared. It began to re-emerge as a city, with people and laughter and life. My sister ran a small bookshop and we shared a small flat situated above the shop near the Marktbrunnen, not far from the Rathaus. I was accepted at the university and studied architecture. For five years we led a very private and happy existence. The war had shattered the nation and its people, but we did our utmost to keep the war out of our tiny flat. We would not talk of it, the war, the deaths, none of that. She would never ask me about the things I saw in Russia. There was the time before the war, and there was *now*, but there was never anything in between. We could not have borne it to be otherwise.

I met Greta Hoffman in Marburg in 1952. She had originally come from Berlin but had fled to the West and finally settled in Marburg after the war had ended. Sometimes I would help my sister run the shop and Greta would come in to buy paper and books. She was very petite, quite shy, and always looked serious, until one day she laughed at a joke my sister told her about us Germans now having to eat paper and books, having to eat our culture because there was so little food. Greta's face was transformed, and as she laughed she looked at me and I at her, and we all laughed, Greta, my sister, and I. In that moment the past was a joke, and in that way we were released from it, if only for a while.

That joke, that shared laughter, made us friends. After that, Greta came to the store every afternoon. She spoke with my sister at first, but then would always talk with me, too. She told me that she loved to read and that she wrote long letters to her cousins, who had fled to America before the war. She had left Berlin because of the bombing and because she had received news of the death of her husband. He had disappeared into the furnace of Stalingrad some time after Christmas, 1942, and like so many other wives and mothers she heard nothing further from him.

My sister saw how my eyes lit up every afternoon when Greta came into the shop. I was a little shy at first, but I began to come out of my shell. My sister said that it was as if I had been dead and was coming back to life again in stops and starts. She joked with me and called me Lazarus. She said that the war had been horrible and men like me often suffered more than others because I was so gentle and kind, and unlike so many others, she said, I had not let myself be transformed into a brute or an animal. By then we knew of the camps, the gassings, and the horrible weight of guilt that the German people bore. My sister believed we bore that guilt collectively and we had to make amends; we had to do good now in this world.

My sister read the newspapers and the articles about the trials at Nürnberg. She was truly horrified. "We are all of us responsible," she said, "because we did nothing to stop this." She said she wanted to atone. I sat every night with her at the dinner table when she spoke. I wondered, how does one atone for Mariupol and Jejsk?

Greta regularly submitted orders for special books or journals, which my sister did her utmost to fill. When the orders came in, my sister sent me off with the package to deliver by hand. I was very nervous at first, not knowing what to say or how to act. But Greta was very kind and very patient and we were friends now. We began going out to cafes together in the evenings or to the cinema sometimes to watch American films. Some were comedies or romances, or stories about the Wild West. I remember one film where cowboys battled Indians in a Nevada desert. They fired at one another and Greta found it quite exciting. She'd squeal if a hero was wounded or in jeopardy and cheer when the Indians were driven off and the day was saved. I never felt that way. I found the gun battles silly, since I knew it was only pretend. In the darkness of the cinema I watched the figures on the big screen and saw how some of the characters would fall and pretend to die. I knew how the dead fell and how they looked afterwards. That was never shown in the movies.

I shed the remnants of an outer skin in Marburg, but the process had begun before I started life anew with my sister and then with Greta. I left that other part of me behind, in the prison camps, with the British intelligence officer, the one with the pale-blue, lifeless eyes. When the kommando crossed the sea from Novorossijsk to the Crimea, a part of me was left behind in Mariupol and in Taganrog, in the wells and the trenches, and in Krasnodar in the cellar where the prisoners burned as we left the city, and where the bodies were hung like ornaments on the lampposts – Fedorov's parting gesture.

I left it all behind. I wanted nothing of my former self to survive that journey. I was in love with Greta. She thought I was kind and sweet and gentle. We never spoke of the war either; only the now and the future could be our concern.

When we married we talked about leaving Germany and emigrating to America, to Canada, where her cousins lived who might act as sponsors.

We submitted many documents and waited for months until finally we were told we must go to Karlsruhe, where our applications would be screened. The Canadian officials had set up a processing centre there, in a large school that looked as if it had been bombed in the war and repaired. We waited there for six hours with dozens of other applicants in a gymnasium. All the while men in uniforms and others in suits buzzed about carrying files and papers. It was very noisy in the gymnasium and one heard the constant clacking of typewriters. Greta and I were interviewed separately. They spent very little time with Greta. They spent much more time with me.

My name was called and I was told to follow a young man from the gymnasium to a small room at the end of a long hallway. We passed many rooms. I could see into some of them, where people were seated at tables while the men in suits and uniforms filled out forms and asked questions. At the end of the hallway the young man knocked on the door and a voice in English said, "Come in."

The young man opened the door and gestured for me to enter. I did and he remained outside and closed the door after me. Inside the room was an older man, quite large, with a black moustache and grey-black hair. He wore a uniform, like a policeman. He spoke German with a thick accent, I thought he was British, Scottish perhaps, but I could not know for sure. He said he was a vetting officer with a branch of the Royal Canadian Mounted Police. He told me that he would have some questions for me, and I was permitted to sit down.

There were many forms that he would have to fill out, some of which I would have to sign afterwards. He looked quite tired. Nevertheless, he was polite. His office was cluttered and jammed with filing cabinets and papers of all sorts. It took some time for him to fill out the forms, and after an hour I thought we were finally finished. There was another form he had to fill out, though. The policeman told me that this form was quite specific and that I had to be absolutely honest in providing my answers. He asked me if I understood. I said that I did.

It was a typed form that contained questions about my service during the war with spaces for the answers. The vetting officer asked me if I had served in the army and with what unit. I told him that I had been an interpreter with the German army on the Eastern Front, but I did not know the name of the unit. His manner seemed to change now: he was less friendly. He looked at me for a moment and I thought of the British officer again, and I began to feel that old fear, the fear of detection, of judgement.

"That seems very odd to me. Why would you not remember the name of your unit?"

I tried to explain that I would interpret for all sorts of units, as a helper, a facilitator, nothing more than that.

"Take your shirt off," he said, his voice curt. I knew what he was looking for now. I did as he ordered, but I had no such tattoo. He examined both my arms and then told me to put my shirt back on. I wanted to run at that moment. I wanted to run back down that hall and take Greta with me and keep running. But I remained in that room and I remained calm.

He asked me more questions about where I had served, but I remained adamant that I was simply an interpreter. I denied knowledge of any killings, of atrocities, of anything of that sort. He continued to question me, though, his voice sharper, more aggressive, but still calm. He was quite practised. He must have questioned many men before: *What kind of uniform did you wear? Who were the other men in your unit? Your officers? Were they SS? Did you carry a weapon?* . . . He wanted names, and places and dates. He wanted to trap me, I think. He wanted me to relent, to stumble, to make a mistake. The room became hotter, oppressive, and seemed to shrink. I feared for Greta and for myself. I thought of the Russians. . . .

I do not know how long the questions continued, except the door to the room opened and another man in a uniform, a soldier, entered. He leaned over and whispered something into the policeman's ear, handed him a second file, looked at me, and then walked out, shutting the door. The policeman opened this second file and appeared to read over its contents. Then he closed the file folder and looked at me with eyes that narrowed. His lips were twisted into a wry grin. He let out a sigh and straightened his body a little. His wooden swivel chair squeaked as he leaned back in it, all the while continuing to look at me.

"Well," he said. "Do you know what this is?" He lifted up a thin folder. It contained some white pages, but I could not see what was written on them.

"No," I said.

"It's your free pass," he said. "The British have a file on you. You've helped them out, Reile, and they're apparently grateful."

His grin faded. His face became darker, his voice now flat and cold.

"This ends the interview. I expect your application will be approved. You and your wife will receive documentation authorizing your entrance into Canada. There your application for citizenship will be processed."

He was looking down at his desk as he spoke. He made a note on a form and said, "Just one minute before you leave." He stood up and walked right up to me. Then he grabbed me by the hair and wrenched my head upwards. His grip was firm. I remained motionless, now in fear for my life. His mouth was inches from my ear and I felt the waves of his breath.

"I don't know exactly what you did, what unit you served with, but there's a stink about you. I saw types like you in Normandy – SS. Pigs, the lot of you, shooting prisoners in the back, just for the fun of it. You've got SS written all over you. That means you're a piece of shite, Reile." He yanked at my hair again and I felt his grip tighten. He twisted my head so we faced one another. His face was red.

"I want you to know this. You're not fooling anyone, not me, not a soul. Before I wore this uniform I was a warrant officer in the Canadian army. One afternoon in July 1944, I walked into a small garden beside a bombed-out house in Normandy. I saw two bodies there, two Canadian soldiers with their hands tied behind their backs and half of their heads taken off from dum-dum bullets put through their skulls. That was the ss at work. We put the word out, though. After that, if one of my lads came across any ss bastards with his hands in the air, shouting, '*Kamerad, Kamerad,*' we took them prisoner, all right – but not until we'd put a bayonet in their belly and cut their throat until it looked like a wide, red grin. I just want you to know that, and here's hoping that one of those fuckers we took care of was your brother or your father or your best friend, you ss coont."

He tossed my head to the side as he let go of my hair. I could not look at him, and I felt ashamed. I could not say this to him, though. He would not want to hear my apologies, not after what he had seen. I sat with my head down. I wondered what type of man I was. A coward, or a monster?

He walked back to his desk and sat down. The chair creaked as he leaned into it.

"Don't forget one other thing, laddie. There's a file on you out there, and it won't go away. It may disappear for a while, but one day it might turn up again, and maybe then you won't have so many friends to protect you."

He told me to get out. I walked down the hall and met Greta in the gymnasium. She had been worried. She stroked my hair because it was messy now and standing on end. I told her everything would be all right. She said I looked very pale. I told her it was only because it had been a very long day.

CHAPTER
SIX

I

———

Viaux called me at work the day he and Digby returned
from Kiev, where they'd been investigating Bock for eight
weeks. The ring of the telephone, a unique event in my
office, made my heart leap.

"I thought you'd moved to Ukraine for good," I said.
"Where are you?"

"At home. We got back yesterday," he said.

"Jesus, why were you guys away so long?"

"It's a long story, I'll come see you this afternoon."

Viaux looked like hell.

"My God," I said. "You've lost twenty pounds!" It was as
if part of him was missing. His shirt, his pants, his blazer were
loose. It was not that he was a fat man. On the contrary, he
was a mountain, firm bulk and muscle, and somehow the loss

of weight was more noticeable in a man of his size. He sat down, and now seemed even smaller. He crossed one leg over the other and folded his hands in front. *Is it possible that even his fingers could have lost weight?*

"Thirty-two," he said. "I caught some sort of bug or virus. I couldn't keep a thing down except bread and bottled water. It's better now," he said. "At least I have my appetite back." He told me he'd eaten poutine for lunch just because it was hot, saturated with fat and salt, and as a result, flavour. His stomach may have rumbled, but as Viaux said, at least there was now something in it.

"And the trip?" I could see from his face that the news would not be good.

"It was a goddamn nightmare," he said. "I'm never going on another trip, not like that one anyway." He looked quite distressed, his bushy eyebrows moving up and down, his tone emphatic. "I wanted to kill Digby by the end."

"Why?"

"Because Digby wanted to do everything his way."

Since the day the SPU opened, numerous lawyers and cops had travelled together on interview trips, and a certain protocol had been established. There were no written rules or anything like that, just a sort of understanding. The idea was that the policeman was supposed to conduct the interviews through an interpreter. Every cop had his own style, but generally he would ask the questions and make a few notes. The interviews were always taped and later transcribed. The lawyers went along to observe the demeanour of the witnesses and maybe throw in a few supplementary questions, test the witness a little, and otherwise just look as if they were awake. Technically, the lawyer was in charge of the interview, but really the cop ran the show. It was a *modus operandi* that normally worked quite well. Viaux had been on at least a dozen trips like this one. He was very bright and very efficient and he didn't believe in wasting time if he wasn't getting any results.

This was Digby's first interview trip, however, and he either didn't understand the protocol or simply chose to ignore it. I suspect the latter. He was well-intentioned, as Viaux said, not witty or entertaining perhaps, but quite affable, and so he should have been an easy travelling companion. Yet I had the impression that behind Digby's affability lay a kind of smugness.

It was as if Digby thought he knew better than anyone else, though he would never come out and actually say that. If I suggested to him that a certain thing had to be done a certain way, I might see his eyes shift a little off to the side and his lips tighten a little, which made me suspect he was thinking otherwise. It was a passive-aggressive trait that made me want to smack him sometimes. Viaux apparently had the same reaction.

"It took two weeks just to interview the first ten people on our list," Viaux said. "I wanted to screen some of them first. You know, talk to them a little, see what they knew or remembered *before* getting into any full-blown interview. That way we wouldn't be wasting time."

I shrugged. "That makes sense."

"Digby wouldn't have any of that. He thought pre-screenings seemed wrong, for some reason, as if we were cutting corners or cheating. He wanted the interviews done in a formal fashion and . . . *in writing*."

I groaned. "But you had a tape recorder."

He unfolded his legs and suddenly moved forward, tapping one finger on my desk as he spoke. "Didn't matter. Digby said it should all be written out, verbatim, every question and every answer, in *both* languages. And he preferred that he ask the questions since he was the lawyer. We averaged one person a day, which would not have been so bad if some of them, even one of them, had something concrete to say."

"Were *any* of them helpful?" I winced, anticipating Viaux's response.

"Short answer? No. You know the problems we're facing here, Dennis. These people are all really old. The youngest was seventy-five. Their memories are dim, they're confused about events and dates and places. None of them knew Bock; they may have heard his name, but they didn't know him. That didn't faze Digby, though. He just kept asking every person the same questions, no matter what their answers."

"What do you mean?"

"I mean he asked *every* person *every* question."

Before their departure, Viaux and I had prepared a list of approximately fifty questions to put to some of the witnesses, depending, of course, on what they said. Some were of a general nature concerning background, while others were more specific: *Did you know Bock? If so, how? Talk to him? See*

him from a distance? Can you describe him? If you didn't know him,
did you know any of the Germans? What kind of uniforms did they
wear, insignias, etc.

Viaux took the list with him to use as a guide or frame-
work. But many of the questions were specifically designed
for persons who might have been familiar with Bock, or at
least some of the men in his unit. Digby didn't see it that
way, though.

"Every single question, Dennis." Viaux paused and
sighed. This was no affectation; he did seem truly exhausted
and exasperated.

"One old guy we spoke to said he was sent to Poland as a
labourer by the Germans in the summer of 1941, so he was
never in Kiev when Bock was there. That was the first thing
he said to us. I thought, okay, end of interview, move on to
the next guy. But Digby didn't stop. 'Did you know any
Germans in Kiev, if so, what were their names?' The guy
replied, 'I didn't know any Germans in Kiev. I was in Poland
for the whole war.' Then Digby asked him, 'Can you describe
the uniforms of any of the Germans you saw in Kiev?' The
poor old guy began to look more and more confused: 'I can't
tell you about any Germans in Kiev. I was in Poland for the
whole war.' Digby again: 'Did you ever hear the name
Heinrich Bock in Kiev during the German occupation?' By
this time the guy must have thought he was crazy, or that
Digby was crazy, or we needed a new translator. I told Digby
this was silly, but he was determined to see it through. I was
too ill to argue by that time anyway. I was dehydrated and
listless. I just did not have the strength. All I could do was sit
there and shrug helplessly."

"My God," I said. I began to rub my right temple. I felt that headache coming on again, that SPU headache. This was not a good thing. It was the "Oh shit" sensation, a sort of unsettling "I am wasting my life" temple-to-temple tremor that rippled through my cranium and throbbed just behind my eyes.

"Did anyone respond to the ads we placed in the Kiev newspapers?" I squinted as I spoke, the throbbing unabated.

"Oh yeah," said Viaux. Another deep sigh, the memory of these recent events apparently still quite painful. "Five people, same story. . . ." He took a deep breath. "I guess Digby thought he was being thorough. I know we have to be diligent and patient in this line of work, but this was plain nonsense. He just wouldn't listen to the answers the people gave. It was as if he refused to accept that they couldn't tell us anything, or he was hoping for some dramatic about-face. . . ." His voice trailed off. Then he leaned forward, about to shed a secret.

"There was something else too."

"What?"

"Isn't Digby married?"

"Last time I heard. Why?" I asked, a little curious.

Viaux snorted. "Then he's going to have to learn to be a little more discreet."

II

It had been two days since I'd spoken with Viaux, and so far Digby hadn't shown his face at the office. But he did arrive unannounced and uninvited at my apartment that evening, looking more dishevelled than ever, and looking almost as rough as Viaux. That's why I'd offered him the drink, *a* drink. Whisky, *single-malt* whisky, was all I had. (He'd sniffed a little at the offer of a glass of wine.) I cursed myself for not having handy a bottle of some cheap blend. I could have done with a tumbler of that stuff. It was more Digby's style.

"My life is in the shitter," Digby said. *No argument here*, I thought.

He was sitting in my living room in one of my shabby old chairs, having just flung another healthy portion of my precious single-malt down his gullet. He put the empty glass on my coffee table, *beside* the coaster, and slid the glass an inch or two in my general direction. That table was the nicest piece of furniture I had, which was not saying much. Digby looked down at the empty glass, then at me, then at the glass again, perhaps a little uncertain why it had not filled itself all on its own with that peaty nectar. I went to the kitchen (a good two yards from the living room), and returned with the rest of the bottle and placed it on the coaster in front of him.

"Help yourself," I said, in a way that suggested *don't* help yourself. He didn't notice my tone or didn't care and poured himself a tumbler's worth. Four fingers, pre-Bock, Viaux-sized fingers, that is.

That bottle of single-malt whisky was a reminder of my last girlfriend, a souvenir. It was a gift from her in celebration of something. Robert Burns? St. Andrew? I don't remember. She would give me gifts like that from time to time when the occasion called for masculine gifts; they were supposed to show that she understood me, as if she really *got* me, and I was supposed to think, how profound, she must really know what I'm all about because she knows I like to drink expensive liquor that someone else has paid for. That was one of the big differences between us, I suppose, and one of the things that drew us apart. She thought, when you loved someone, that you became a part of them, that you came to understand them and know them, that you captured them in a way, as they captured you. I felt we were together because we just happened to be together and that we could just as easily be apart. You can try to connect to someone as much as you want, no one really knows anyone anyway.

But I did know a little about whisky and the bottle, and more importantly, the whisky had hung around longer than she had. I had connected with *that*. I had also been sensitive to the grandeur of that particular stock. I never guzzled it; I preserved it quite successfully, allowing myself a dribble or two on a special occasion, treasuring it, savouring it, respecting it. It was real sipping stuff, meant to be nursed and coddled and gently coaxed over one's lips. I guess she really *did* get me; she just didn't realize it at the time.

At any rate, all remnants of that woman were washed away as Digby flung another large glassful down his throat. He sniffed a little and looked around my living room. In five years of living here I hadn't done a lot with the place. I had hung a few pictures on the wall, a couple of framed art posters; the rest of the place was filled mostly with books and papers and my sprawling collection of compact discs, mostly campus-radio stuff that everyone now called alternative rock.

Watching Digby, all rumpled and messy, a mascot for the absolutely wretched, I was forced to reflect upon my system of beliefs for a moment. I don't believe in a lot of things. I think families are overrated, for example. And I resent earnest platitudes and folksy homilies which are purposely generalized, conveniently imprecise, making them sneaky and misleading. And I will not suffer that "everything happens for a reason" crap either. Years ago, I had a girlfriend in my first year of university who was always saying that. *Everything happens for a reason.* It was a mantra to guide and comfort her through the tremendous hardship of her college days spent skipping classes and hanging out at the Moon and Stars Cafe. (I spoiled it for her, though, by getting drunk at her Summer Solstice party and telling her that everything was just as likely to happen for a bad reason as a good one, or indeed for no reason at all. She broke up with me after that, saying I was just like Ted Hughes.)

I do hang my hat on one general rule: NOTHING IS EVER AS BAD AS IT SEEMS. The rule is not absolute. I will concede there are rare exceptions to the rule, but they remain, nevertheless, rare. And one of those rarities was camped out on my couch slurping back my single-malt and beginning to blubber.

Digby had made a mistake, had a lapse in judgement, a moment of non-lucidity. To be more precise, he had fucked around on his wife and been caught and summarily kicked out of his house. Every evening in Kiev, almost from the start, while Viaux huddled and shivered in his bug-infested room, his feverish mind relishing a variety of scenarios having the commonality of Digby's death, Digby would retire to the welcoming arms, and the bed, of Sondra the translator.

"What was I thinking?" he said, the tedious refrain of all cheating husbands, exasperated by his own stupidity and unable to pinpoint the reason behind his infidelity.

"That's the point, Digby, I don't think you *were* thinking." I'm afraid I wasn't much help, though I was supplying the single-malt.

I'd never met Sondra, but I understood she was a competent translator. She was Dutch, living in The Hague, and fluent in German, Russian, Ukrainian, and, of course, English. She was regularly hired by the SPU whenever it sent investigative parties overseas. Digby told me he'd found her irresistible from the moment they met, that there was something very earthy, sensual, alluring about her that he could not resist or even explain. He pulled out a crumpled photograph from his jacket pocket and handed it to me. She was blonde, quite pleasant looking, with a pretty smile, pink round cheeks, and wide muscular shoulders. A little plump perhaps, with short hair in a boyish cut. She had a kind of sporty look, as if she should always be wearing hiking boots, or jogging along forest trails.

"I thought I loved her. She, on the other hand, wanted to be very *practical* about the whole thing." He said that word, *practical*, with a kind of wounded disdain, worthy of any would-be pale, wan, fond, and rebuked lover. "She said she thought I was very sweet but too serious. She had a husband, the aristocrat, the rich diplomat, in The Hague."

He sniffed, "She told me she did not want me to be *serious*, she wanted me to be *discreet*." He gave me his hurt look of incredulity, crinkling his eyes a little and shaking his head, re-emphasizing his disbelief. Lovesick, he poured a little more peat juice down his gullet.

I looked at him with a guileless, sympathetic glance while I thought about his predicament: *Let me get this straight: she gave you love-free, guilt-free, no-cost, no-strings, great recreational sex, in return asking only that you keep your mouth shut – and now you're bitter because she won't chuck Baron Von Diplomat of The Hague on a whim for the sake of a hapless married guy living five thousand miles away in the capital city of a cultural wasteland?* The woman *was* a catch, a wise woman. Then again, I always equated wisdom with the worldly. That meant she was realistic and pragmatic and therefore wholly unsuited for Digby.

Digby said that they had parted company at the international airport in Vienna, where they had a three-hour stopover between connecting flights. She was flying back to her home in Amsterdam, near where her husband resided. Digby thought perhaps Sondra and her better half had a kind of understanding. One of those European things, he assured me. They had one final embrace, one final long kiss. "One long, deep kiss," he said, his eyes drifting a little, suggesting he was travelling back in time, to a scene in Vienna, at the airport, the resolution predictable. "After that, after that kiss, she was gone, and that would be the end of it."

Except Digby has the worst luck in the world. Events and circumstances beguile us, overwhelm us, and leave us reeling and far behind. While Digby was lost in that final kiss, Sondra's very active tongue disabusing any onlooker of the notion the pair could be anything but lovers, Bryndyce's venerable schoolmates, Gretchen and Karl, happened by, having worn out their welcome in yet another world capital, glumly returning home to their own in Switzerland.

"I never saw them," Digby said, "but they saw me, kissing Sondra."

Digby figured that Gretchen, with the swiftness that only schadenfreude could summon, called Bryndyce – *collect*, of course – from the Vienna International Airport. Bryndyce, appreciative of the call, had the locks to their house changed while Digby and Viaux were still soaring above the Atlantic. Now she was threatening divorce, and threatening to tell Goreman that Digby had been screwing the hired help, and all because of an investigation that seemed to be going nowhere.

"I can't be divorced," he said. "It was my fault, but I was enraptured, possessed. I can't explain why I did it; it just happened." He was on the verge of tears again, so I handed him a Kleenex. He wondered if I might talk to Bryndyce on his behalf, explain it to her, that he'd only screwed around a little, not a lot. It was just this one time. I told him that might not be the best way to earn her forgiveness.

"Give her a little time," I said. "She'll come around." I

said this with conviction, my voice soft, earnest, and replete with understanding.

This seemed to make him feel better. He nodded. "Yeah, you're right, she'll cool down. She just needs time." He groaned and wavered a little as he stood up and negotiated the two yards or so to the door.

"Well, I gotta go." His speech was a little slurred. "*Man!*" he shouted, remembering, perhaps Vienna, Kiev, or the fact he had to spend the night in a hotel. "Fucking Gretchen! I hate the Swiss."

"I just hate," I said.

He looked at me, his eyes a little out of focus, and nodded as if I'd just said something quite profound.

He left, and I watched from my window as he made his way a little shakily up Metcalfe Street towards his hotel. I felt a little bad because I didn't believe for one second that Bryndyce just needed time; she'd had all the time she needed to make up her mind, in the time it takes to say, "Yes, operator, I'll accept the collect call." She did not strike me as the forgiving kind, though I could be wrong, of course. She'd probably tell Goreman about the affair, too, just as she threatened. Digby didn't seem to care about that part, but I would have if I were him. A little titbit like that would cost him his job.

Every rule, even my rules, has its exception. Sometimes things are definitely worse than you think they ever could be.

III

____

I didn't tell Digby that, at the moment, my life was going
quite well. This has to be put into a certain context. When it
comes to wondering what joys life will bring, I believe in
having low expectations. Such a perspective ensures that the
inevitable disappointments are easier to absorb. Even so, for
the moment, life was rather grand.

In the few short weeks since Elizabeth had been assigned
to the Reile file with me, she and I had moved from being
co-workers to acquaintances, to friends, to dates, to regular
visitors in one another's bed. As if that were not enough, a
few days before Digby's world was to come crashing down
around him, Goreman had come into my office with a letter
in his hand that would permit Elizabeth and me to fly to
Moscow and then to Rostov-on-Don.

Goreman placed the letter on my desk.

It was from the procurator in Rostov-on-Don responding to a letter above Goreman's signature I had sent eight
months before seeking confirmation on the status of a group
of eleven persons tried and convicted in 1963 for collaborating with the Nazis after the German invasion of the Soviet
Union. The Soviets had allowed the SPU access to some of
the trial records. All of those tried had implicated Reile,

among others, in a series of mass executions in the Black Sea region of Russian and Ukraine. Though it was likely that all eleven persons tried had been subsequently executed, I'd submitted the letter regardless.

The procurator's letter confirmed that ten of the eleven had been executed in 1963, but the eleventh, Sikorenko, was in good health and residing near Rostov-on-Don. He had served thirty years in the Gulag and was now free. He now worked as a carpenter. Of the eleven, Sikorenko had had the most to say about Reile. The records of his statements to the KGB investigators was pretty damning stuff.

I said, "This looks promising."

"Let's hope so," he said.

Since I was the most familiar with the file, Goreman wanted me to go to Rostov-on-Don. He thought we didn't need to send a police investigator, because Elizabeth was experienced in criminal prosecutions. He wanted us both to get over there as soon as we could. I told Elizabeth that same afternoon and we went out to celebrate at a restaurant and then later in her bedroom. Life was simple and getting sweeter.

It took a couple of weeks to book flights, requisition money advances, and obtain our visas. Our interpreter would be Rita Taschenko, who had worked with me on several occasions in Minsk and Kiev, translating Russian documents held at various archives. She was very happy to hear from me when I called, and though she always spoke very formally, there was a sincerity and a warmth behind her words. She was divorced and lived in a small apartment in Moscow with her five-year-old daughter and her brother Levin, a former soldier who now worked as a chauffeur. I hired him as our driver. They could be available as early as the first day of October. As usual I told Rita to give me a list of things she wanted me to bring: toys, books, and maybe a little whisky for Levin, who liked a nip or two.

Elizabeth and I arrived in Moscow via Frankfurt on October 3, 1993. Rita was there to meet us after we had cleared customs. She greeted us warmly, hugging us both with little pecks on our cheeks, then quickly ushered us outside to Levin's waiting automobile. He gave me a nod as we climbed in, having stuffed our luggage into the trunk. Levin was gloomier than ever, as if a dark aura hovered permanently about him.

"You have arrived at a rather unfortunate time," Rita said, in her formal way. As she spoke a voice came over the car radio announcing, in English, that Boris Yeltsin had declared martial law. Rita explained that some renegades in the Russian parliament had instigated an uprising of sorts, and incidents of violence had broken out in several parts of the city. The voice also said that the airport was now closed for departing flights.

"What does this mean?" Elizabeth asked. She was looking to me, even though Rita had been speaking to us both.

"It means we will not be flying to Rostov tomorrow, but we must wait and see," Rita said. "Perhaps we can fly the day after. We'll get you settled at the hotel first."

The evening sky was darkening as we sped from the airport into Moscow along a wide boulevard, the main route into the city. I recognized this same sky, having been here once, three years before. Rita and I had spent a week at a KGB archive in downtown Moscow. Although access to the

archive was limited to certain parts of the building, I was permitted to pore over a cache of Gestapo and SS files captured
by the Russians in Berlin, and bundled up and taken to
Moscow shortly after the war. I remember the papers in each
file were very stiff, the typewritten letters of each page set
out in a heavy, severe font. German, and yet still very foreign,
as if not of this world. My German was passable and I knew
enough to identify any documents that might be of assistance
to SPU files. Attached to each file was a Soviet report in
Cyrillic script which Rita would translate for me and write
out in longhand.

The road was wide, three lanes. I looked out the window
at the sky again. It was like the skies I saw as a boy in
Winnipeg in the fall: pale, endless, seamless, a tremendous
expanse, with the smell of woodsmoke in the air. To the side
of the roadway I saw dismal shapes in the distance, factories
and ugly concrete apartment buildings, all pre-fab and crum-
bling. Levin spoke to Rita in Russian and pointed to a spot
off the highway. I was familiar with the monument. The first
time I had seen it was three years before. It had left a deep
impression upon me. I saw it again, large, tall, with black
girders in a three-dimensional X, a monument shaped as a
giant tank-trap. It marked a spot fourteen kilometres from
the centre of the city.

"What is it?" Elizabeth asked me, her voice higher, anticipating my reply. She pressed her face a little against the car
window to get a better view.

"It marks the farthest advance of the German army into
Moscow. An advance unit made it this far before it was
pushed back."

It stood, like Moscow, rusted in spots, decrepit, a little neglected. Still, it stood. Nothing could change what had happened here, no matter how much time had passed. It was odd, though, since I always felt that the monument had an ambiguous quality, albeit unintentionally. Its simplicity conveyed a sense of the pitiful, the poignant, and the heroic. It gave me a sense of history, that tremendous things had occurred here, in this suburb of Moscow that now seemed little more than a squalid series of apartment complexes and closed factories and waste. And yet, though the monument purported to immortalize the brave defenders of Moscow, I could not help but think of the tiny German patrol that had made it this far, like the tip of a finger at the end of an outstretched arm, the men in the patrol almost able to see the lights of the Kremlin before being driven back. Then the winter had set in. General January. After that, time and the inevitable weighed against them. Time was not on the side of the Germans. It led to retreat and ignominy. And so the monument still stood, in remembrance of both sides of that story.

As we moved farther into the city, we could see shops and office buildings and apartments. A streetcar line ran parallel to the wide road we were travelling on. I could see the dark forms of commuters, some getting off, some lined up to get on the shabby blackened cars. Along the side of the wide street, forms moved about in a mass, shoppers carrying knitted shopping bags, silhouetted against the dim lights of streetlamps and empty-looking stores. A brown haze hung over the city and everyone in it, as if all were coated in an ubiquitous grime.

We arrived at our hotel, which was quite opulent and brightly lit inside, a dramatic contrast to the gloom outside. Staff and bellboys scurried about. We were told that there was an evening curfew of nine o'clock. Rita offered to stay a few minutes to see that we were properly checked in, but I told her that she and Levin should hurry home, before the curfew. Levin waved from inside the car and then they were off.

"This is very exciting," Elizabeth said, looking almost surprised to learn that something interesting might actually occur.

We were standing beside the counter, being checked into our rooms. A bellboy stood nearby, guarding a trolley with our luggage piled atop. Apparently neither of us was adept at packing light, since between us we had six large pieces of luggage for a planned one-week trip.

"What does this curfew mean for us?" she asked me, her brows furrowed, very curious. Her skin was quite clear, almost translucent, and she wore little, if any, make-up today – because we were travelling, I suppose. I thought that she was quite beautiful here. She looked different than in Ottawa, at work. Today she looked more natural, less adorned. I can't explain it. She didn't even look tired, though we'd been travelling for almost eighteen hours.

"Are we stuck here, do you think? Will be we spending Christmas in the Gulag?" She seemed to be enjoying every minute of this, as if it were a great adventure. Her pleasure was infectious and my fatigue did not prevent my feeling the same way. There was tension in the air, a sense of excitement, a sense of being part of something bigger than oneself. I thought again of the monument fourteen kilometres outside

Moscow. It was rather like that, the sense that we were being subsumed by a greater whole.

We checked into separate rooms, but that was essentially a formality.

"I'm having a shower and washing my hair," she said. "I'll be over at your room in an hour or so." I hoped she would hurry.

My room was large and clean. The hotel was obviously new, apparently owned by a German company. I turned on the television and watched CNN for a while and saw the replay from earlier in the afternoon of a demonstration at the Garden Ring that had turned into a riot. It all seemed rather remote, rather removed from me and my world. There was also a report on the Ostankino TV station that dozens were killed in an attack by the renegades.

An hour later Elizabeth knocked at my door, her face still glowing a little from the heat of her shower, her hair tied back. I felt a rumpled mess in comparison. She kissed me.

"Great rooms," she said, looking about. "I expected much worse."

"So did I," I yawned. "This is a new hotel, I've usually stayed closer to downtown." I had almost dozed off in front of the television.

"Let's go eat," she said. "I'm famished."

We ate a light dinner in one of the hotel restaurants, the curfew now in effect. It was quite crowded, of course, and noisy, so we didn't stay long. She said we should leave.

"I have a bottle of wine in my suitcase," she said, lowering her voice a little, "for emergencies and, I suppose, given the day's events, *curfews*. Let's have a glass in your room and then have dessert." She whispered the words and widened her eyes a little, a look that was both suggestive and ironic all at once. In that one expression she captured the essence of our relationship. When I think back on those few months that we were together, there was always a sense of newness, of novelty. I remember the moments of lovemaking, her lips, her hair, her soft skin, the warmth of her, the energy in those moments that flowed from her and into me, and from me into her. She was like no one else I had ever known.

It was that newness that drew me to her, that made me crave her. She was a delightful mystery to be explored, though only to a certain extent. I had no desire to learn everything about her. That would spoil it all. I wanted to learn just enough so that when the time came I would miss her. She told me that first day, at the SPU, that in a few months she'd be gone. I understood that. She understood that. That was the unspoken deal. In Moscow, in my hotel room, she looked at me with bright eyes and said she wanted me, and I said that I wanted her. And so, as before in Ottawa, we would make love, always conscious of a clock ticking in our background. That did not sadden us, it made the moments we shared much more precious. As Elizabeth and I embarked upon this journey through Moscow to explore the past, I felt deeply conscious of the present, savoured it, delighted in it, knowing how swiftly it would be absorbed by the inexorable mechanism of time that reduces future to present and swiftly to past.

As I slept, I dreamed of explosions and the sound of gunfire. Then Elizabeth woke me. She had grabbed my arm and tried to shake me a little.

"Wake up!" she said. "Something is happening." She was standing beside the bed, dressed in a T-shirt and jeans. Her hair was damp and I could see she had just had a shower.

The television was on, CNN, and I saw several tanks moving along a street, then seeming to stop and position themselves on a large street near to what was described as the parliament building in Moscow. Some helicopters circled in the air above. There were other armoured vehicles, too, moving in a column along the downtown Moscow streets, and I saw groups of soldiers and police standing about. I could see that crowds of people, civilians, had gathered, their numbers increasing.

"What time is it?" I asked. My voice was hoarse.

"It's almost eight," she said, still staring at the television and putting on a pair of socks. Then she fastened her belt and I heard the sound of a zipper as she did up her jeans. "You know, we can't miss this. We have to get down there!" She said this as if she had just made a decision, and I could not tell if she was speaking to me or herself. She was still sitting at the end of the bed, tucking a corner of her shirt down the back of her jeans, and I caught a glimpse of her white underwear. When she turned her head to look at me I had already sat up and moved down the bed, close behind her, naked beneath the warm layers of sheets and blankets. I began to kiss the back of her neck.

Unlike her, at this moment I did not see the tanks, nor the troops, nor the convoys of armoured vehicles. I saw

nothing of the threat of civil war and unrest, of riots and
bloodshed and chaos. I simply saw Elizabeth's long legs in
tight jeans, and the way her cream-coloured T-shirt accen-
tuated the darker shape of her breasts underneath. I thought
of how she was with me a few hours before. I kissed her
long white neck and felt the dampness of her hair. I moved
my hands down from her shoulders along the curve of her
breasts and my fingers felt their way to the firmness of
her. . . . *Alas, no luck this morning.*

She arched her back a little like a cat and said very firmly,
"We don't have time." She was smiling, though, as she turned
to push me away. She pushed me backwards onto the bed and
straddled my chest, pinning my arms. She moved her face
close to mine. Her eyes shone as she frowned again. "Come
on! We have to go down there, to the parliament buildings.
This is one of those moments. You read about these things in
the papers and you wish you were there to see what happened. We're in the right place at the right time. Let's make
the most of it!" She got off me and sat beside me as I still lay
in bed. "This could be something big. Let's go and see, try to
be a part of it! Of *something*." She was pleading a bit now.
"We can't go to Rostov, not today anyway. The airport is
closed. What else is there to do?" She was nodding, her eyes
pleading again.

I could not resist her arguments. She pretended to sound
exasperated, but I knew behind the joking and the pretend
pleading there lay a will, and I saw the intensity of her gaze
fixed upon the images on the screen. I imagined that was
how she must look in court, when she prosecuted her cases;
intense, focused, shutting out everything else. It was the look

she had sometimes when we made love. Sometimes she would ask me to leave the lights on so we could see one another, so we weren't simply groping around in the dark, reaching out for our own pleasures. And she was right about Rostov. The night before, Rita had left a message telling me the airport would be closed for at least another day, and Rostov was too far away to drive.

"I need to have a shower first," I grumbled. I threw back the covers and sheets and shuffled in the direction of the bathroom and shower. Her eyes were still glued to the television.

"Okay," she said. "I'll go get my jacket while you shower." She passed me on the way out and kissed me on the mouth. I smelled her hair and skin and reached up again with my fingers, trying to delve beneath the cream-coloured T-shirt. She rapped my hands.

"Later," she said. "The civil war's not going to wait! You're a historian, you're supposed to be into this sort of thing!" She dashed out the door and I settled for a long, hot shower. The civil war could bloody well wait a few more minutes before it erupted.

We managed to get a taxi from the lobby. The drive took us to within a kilometre or so of the Ukraine Hotel and we walked the rest of the way, following the streams of people heading in that direction. On the street, crowds of onlookers had gathered. There were soldiers, too, and police, and more armoured vehicles. Barriers were being set up to contain the growing crowds. I saw several large white vans with satellite equipment on their roofs and nearby television cameras, perched upon platforms, were aimed in the direction of the white parliament buildings, still almost a kilometre in the distance.

It was a chilly morning, but the air was clear and the sky brightening. As we worked our way into the crowd I took Elizabeth's hand. "I don't want to be separated," I said. We passed the hotel on the Kalinina Prospect and moved farther along with the crowd, closer to the parliament building, crossing the Kalininsky Bridge over the Moscow River. We were wrapped up in it all, the excitement of it, the sense of danger and wonder. All about us, people were chattering excitedly amidst the smell of tobacco and diesel fumes and smoke.

We looked upwards at the parliament building, in which several hundred people had barricaded themselves. We were standing only a few hundred yards from it when the first shells crashed into it several storeys up, and the sound of the blasts shot through my body like a giant fist of air. Arms, shoulders, knees struck against me as the people around us began to scramble back the way they'd come. Elizabeth was shoved sideways and tumbled down to the pavement on her hands and knees. Another shell crashed into the building, higher up this time, near the top. I saw the burst of light and flame, then heard the blast and saw white dust fall from the hole the shell had made, while black smoke poured upwards. People were fleeing now that the shooting had begun. Their bodies passed in front of me, over me, shoving me aside, but I managed to fling myself down towards Elizabeth, where she struggled to get up, looking stunned and confused by the suddenness of it all.

After this last shell hit the building, the air was suddenly filled with the sharp whooshing sound of bullets rushing past our heads. "They're shooting!" I yelled at Elizabeth, and grabbed her arm to haul her up. We ran several yards, hunched over almost double, throwing ourselves in against a short, wide wall that separated the road from a pedestrian way. A group of at least fifty other people were huddled along that same wall. I heard more bullets whistle overhead. I had pressed Elizabeth in against the wall and lay over her. Some other people crashed into us as they leapt for cover. There was more shooting, seemingly from everywhere, popping sounds that echoed and ricocheted.

There were more blasts from the tanks, and I could see they were moving up the road towards us. The pavement beneath us shook, and I felt the force of the soundwaves from the blast. The shooting stopped, and the crowd was up again and running towards the tanks. We followed and scrambled with the others across a concrete embankment and then along another street. Several soldiers had run towards us from the direction of the tanks, yelling at us in Russian, urging us to keep running while pointing to an area behind a row of armoured vehicles. A great burly soldier wearing a beret and a thick short coat grabbed our arms, hauling us with him until we reached a wooden barricade about a hundred yards farther down the street. Then he let go and ran back up the street to grab other stragglers and take them to safety. He reminded me of Viaux, just the size of him and the wide face with the trimmed grey and white moustache.

We stood there at the wooden traffic barricade, witless, stunned and mute, staring up at the white parliament building. My heart pounded, my body throbbed from the waves of adrenaline. Black smoke streamed in columns from some of the windows; flashes of tracer rounds, like shooting stars, went hurtling across the sky, hitting the exterior walls and exploding, sending fragments upwards and outwards until they fell many storeys to the street below. Roars, bursts, noise, encasing us as if by a wall of sound.

At the barricade, we were safe now, but still overwhelmed by the intensity of those few seconds. "Are you all right?" I could barely speak to Elizabeth as I struggled to catch my breath. She nodded.

Then I saw the blood soaking through the knees of her jeans, and the thin stream of blood running down one arm.

"Jesus!" I said, thinking she'd been hit by a bullet or some fragment.

Her face was very pale suddenly, and I thought she was going to faint. She looked down at her knees and at her arm for a second, but seemed to regain her composure. Then she started to laugh.

"It's all right," she said. "Look." She raised her arm to show me her bleeding elbow. "It's from the pavement." Then she looked back up at the white building. Her face turned white again, but her eyes were filled with dark intensity, wonder and fear at the same time, rapt in a way. "It's horrible and beautiful all at once."

I knew what she meant and I stared, too, seeing black smoke against the white of the building. It was shattered in places, pocked, gouged, and dark inside. The sound of automatic weapons from within the building seemed to intensify as the attackers moved upwards, floor by floor, and the resistance flagged. I felt quite small now, overwhelmed by what had just happened.

I pulled some tissue out of the pocket of my jacket and pressed the wad of it against the cut on her elbow. One of the knees of her jeans was torn, but the blood had begun to dry, forming a dark stain on the denim. We stood side by side for several hours in the same spot, amongst hundreds of others who'd come to watch the terrible spectacle. The crowd was silent, though, as we watched the flames and smoke continue to pour from the windows. The sound of automatic weapons continued, subsiding for a while, then reaching a crescendo, and then subsiding again. The sky seemed very clear, pale with shades of blue and red as the first traces of dusk began to fall. The sounds of the battle still echoed and bounced off the walls of the surrounding city buildings, at once coming from everywhere and nowhere.

Late in the afternoon, we arrived at the lobby of our hotel, where I guided Elizabeth over to a sitting area with couches and chairs. We stared blankly at one another for a moment. She looked very pale again and quite frightened, as if the quiet aftermath of the afternoon turned to evening caused her to reflect on the violence of the morning's events.

"I'm still getting over the shock," I said, almost in a whisper, and shook my head a little. "What the hell were we thinking?" Then I began to laugh, without intending to, and she began to laugh too. The fear we had felt had held us in its grip until something within said enough is enough. Our laughter spilled over into paroxysms of hysterical giggling. We collapsed onto a big wide couch, our eyes wide and filled with tears, the waves of laughter feeling like spasms of pain and pleasure that eventually subsided. I sat back in the couch to look at her, her beautiful face, long, a little thin, but full of colour and light again.

We sat there for a few seconds, catching our breath. Nearby, a woman in a hotel uniform had set up a table with glasses and was now filling them with champagne. Apparently we had arrived in time for the complimentary champagne hour.

"Oh, God," Elizabeth said, a look of relief still passing over her face as she regained her composure, "what a tremendous idea."

I brought over two glasses and handed her one for a toast.

"To us," she said. "That's the best I can come up with at the moment."

We both took tremendous gulps and agreed a second round was needed. I walked over to the table where the woman was still pouring champagne into the glasses. She was quite dark and young and had a very striking face, with high cheekbones, and she smiled as I approached. She had seen us giggling on the couch, Elizabeth bloodied, me also looking rather the worse for wear. She placed a newly opened bottle on a tray with two full glasses. "Take this instead," she said, still smiling, her voice deep and richly accented. "You both look like you have earned it." She laughed, and refused the tip I offered.

We sat in that lobby for a long time, drinking the entire bottle. I felt the pleasure and the warmth of that effervescent liquid flow through me. The day had softened now. Elizabeth lay back to look at me, contented, a little drunk perhaps. Then she moved forward and placed her open palms on my cheeks. Her eyes closed as she opened her mouth so slightly and kissed me. I could taste the sweetness of the champagne on her lips. Her cheeks were warm and flushed. She said, "Let's go to our room."

We lay together in my bed as she slept, her body pressed against mine. I felt the warmth of her and the softness of her hair. In the silence and the darkness I closed my eyes and the flashing brilliant images of the day whirled about my head and then subsided. I felt very tired now. Hours before, the shooting, the bullets, the explosions had left me shocked, feeling exposed and helpless, acutely aware that my continued existence was a tenuous, unpredictable condition, a product of circumstance.

At the end of this day we laughed and drank and made love, clinging to one another, her arms and legs holding me tight against her, as I held her against me. We celebrated because, despite our foolishness, we were alive. I think we were both living for the day, the moment, not thinking about the future. This day could have gone horribly wrong, but it hadn't, and that reassured me somehow. As I was falling asleep, I felt safe again.

Rita called me at eight the next morning. She said that she had made some inquiries at the airport.

"The airport is closed for one more day, perhaps two," she said. "And it is impossible to make a telephone call to

Rostov. Everything is jammed up because of all the trouble. I think I will have better luck tomorrow, though. Things will have settled down by then. Did you watch the television yesterday?"

I said that I had.

"It was horrible, simply horrible, and shameful too! What a nation we have become! What the world must think of us now!" She was so earnest when she spoke, and after hearing her I was too ashamed to tell her that Elizabeth and I had rushed down to the heart of the city, *her city*, to watch it all unfold. Rita was older than I, perhaps thirty-seven or thirty-eight, and she was of a generation of Russians brought up in the shadow of that legacy of the Great Patriotic War. On her wedding day she and her husband had followed a well-observed tradition and paused at the torch that burned at the memorial site outside the walls of the Kremlin, commemorating the sacrifice of the millions who had died in defence of her country. She would not have been impressed that we had treated this recent spate of violence, this highly contained set-piece skirmish, this burst of civil war as a spectator sport.

"So," she said, her English very formal, but her voice very warm, a mother's voice, a caring voice, "I will call you tomorrow at this same time and hopefully we can leave for Rostov. I tried to call the room of Elizabeth but there was no answer," she added. I said that she had probably gone for a jog or something, feeling Elizabeth's small fist strike my hip as she covered her head with her pillow and groaned, indicating a desire to sleep many more hours. Rita said that

Elizabeth should be careful: she was not in Canada now, and Moscow streets were no longer as safe as they were before *glasnost*.

"So we're stuck here for at least another day?" Elizabeth said, decidedly more energetic after two more hours of sleep and a long hot bath. She was now polishing off a very generous plate of eggs Benedict, blinis, and toasted muffins.

We were seated in one of the hotel restaurants that offered an immense breakfast buffet, and she had filled her plate to the edges. "I know," she said, "I'm eating like a pig, but I'm famished. I have never been so hungry!" I enjoyed watching her eat, looking content, relaxed, and barely smoking, too. I saw a change in her today.

In the weeks since she began work with us I could see that a cloud hung over her, or perhaps there was a kind of darkness about her. She was a litigator, she said, and she could not bear to spend each day simply sitting in an office waiting for the day that a suspect may or may not ever be indicted.

The difference between us, of course, was that I was at the SPU by choice and she was not. And, notwithstanding all the frustrations and the disappointments, I still believed in the work of the SPU. Despite my cynicism, despite my jaded views on just about everything else, I still believed that something could be done. Elizabeth had no such faith. She felt that she was in exile. For her it was simply a question of putting in time. She had to feel that she was accomplishing something, and the SPU offered her no such opportunities.

Today was different.

"So," she said, moving back her plate, scraped clean, and now stirring a cup of coffee, "what is the plan with Sikorenko?"

"What do you mean?" I asked. I had almost forgotten about him, given everything that had happened the day before.

She was rocking a little in her chair, as if energized. "Well, we have to have a plan, a strategy. How do we approach this guy? Should we be nice to him, aggressive, what?" She was looking at me intently, wanting answers. "We want to get a good statement from him."

"You're quite keen today," I said. I was a little dubious as I stirred my coffee and picked at a piece of toast.

"It's just that I feel so inspired now, so energized. Do you know what I mean?"

"Because of what happened yesterday?"

"Yes, of course, but it's more than that." She drew her hair back with her hands, letting the curls flow out from between her fingers. She frowned, her lips closing a little, her eyes narrowing slightly before she spoke. "I never told you about what happened in Toronto. It's not something I'm proud of. I told you that I screwed up and that I made a mistake. Now it's like I have an opportunity to redeem myself, to get my life back on track."

"What happened in Toronto?" I asked. She had alluded to this incident many times.

"I was assisting another prosecutor on a murder trial and one of my tasks was to ensure that the defence attorney was fully apprised of the evidence the prosecution had against his client. The term for it is disclosure."

She took a sip of her coffee and grimaced. "Stay away from the coffee." She reached down to the floor and pulled a cigarette out of her purse and lit it.

"The case was pretty straightforward. The accused had stabbed his girlfriend to death at her apartment after they'd had a fight in the middle of the afternoon. The neighbours heard the yelling in the hallway of the apartment and saw the accused running past and heading for the exit. He was arrested the next day."

"Sounds pretty strong," I said. I reached for my cup of coffee then remembered her warning.

"There was one wrinkle. This woman, this *meddler*, who had no connection to the accused, was convinced she saw him at her favourite video store on the other side of the city at the time of the killing."

"Uh-oh."

"No, no, no," she said with impatience. "She was wrong about the date. The police checked with the video store. She'd seen him the week before."

"What was the problem then?"

"The police took a statement from her and . . ." She hesitated and looked down at her cup. "I forgot to send it to the defence attorney. I was stupid, sloppy. She was not an alibi, we could prove that, but I was obliged to send her statement and I overlooked it."

"How did it come out?"

"A few days after the trial started. The senior prosecutor had me in his office and asked me what the fuck I was doing screwing up his case. He took me off the case, a mistrial was declared, and I was sent to the Gulag for nine months as punishment for my sins. So you can see why this interview with Sikorenko is so important to me. It's a chance to break open this case. That trial in Toronto shook me up and robbed me of my confidence. This is a chance to redeem myself. I'm good at what I do; I want to prove it."

The next day Rita made the call from my hotel room to the procurator in Rostov-on-Don to confirm our arrival and arrange a time to interview Sikorenko. She did not speak for long and the expression on her face did not suggest the news was good. After she hung up, she said that the procurator was quite upset. "He said, 'But Sikorenko is dead! You are too late! He died two months ago, a stroke. I advised your embassy of this fact in writing two days after he died.'" Rita said the procurator was very impatient with her and rude. "'Tell the Canadians that there have been one hundred murders in my oblast this year alone. I don't have the men or the resources to handle the crimes of the present, to say nothing of the past!'"

I looked over at Elizabeth who had been sitting at a writing table in my room. She covered her face with her hands and shook her head. There was no place to go now but home.

IV

We were jammed into economy class awaiting departure from Frankfurt. The overhead bins were full, so our feet rested atop our carry-on bags. My knees had already begun to throb. From where I was seated I could see into the first-class and business-class sections. They were rather more spacious, due to the fact that virtually none of the seats were occupied. In one row a pair of off-duty flight attendants settled in for the flight and sipped on their pre-flight cocktails. Once we were airborne a curtain was drawn, blinding my view of that other world. It would have been simpler to dash through Checkpoint Charlie in the Cold War days than to get through that curtain.

"Well, that was a bit of a bust," Elizabeth said bitterly. She yawned, then scowled as she looked out the window. "Couldn't someone have told us just a bit sooner?" We were an hour into the flight and had yet to see so much as a pretzel or a cocktail napkin. "I mean, honestly," she said, "how complicated is it to send one lousy letter from Moscow to Ottawa? No wonder we can't catch any Nazis. We can't even keep track of our own stupid correspondence. *God*, how did I get myself into this mess?" She spoke to the window, but the window did not reply.

We had called the embassy from our hotel and the procurator was right. He had sent the letter right away and it was received at the embassy, but there was a shortage of staff and somebody had been on holidays. The letter got stalled somewhere in the limbo between in-trays and out-trays.

"I don't know what to say." I was bitter too. It was more than just Sikorenko's death that disheartened me. I thought about the melee at the parliament building, the dead, the sense of chaos and uncertainty. And I thought about what the procurator had said: we *were* too late, and now he had much more pressing concerns. The events of the present were overwhelming those of the past, and I felt rather irrelevant at the moment, as if I was simply an observer who had nothing meaningful to contribute.

My eyes remained fixed on the drawn curtain, my nose and throat dry from inhaling the same stale bacteria-laden air that they'd pumped through the plane since the moment we took off. My right knee was in agony, my feet swollen, resembling watermelons with laces. A child, who apparently was being tortured in the row behind me in the presence of oblivious parents, was screaming with an intensity and pitch that made me wish this transit bus of an airplane might plunge the thirty thousand or so feet required to reach the surface of the Atlantic at an angle and speed sufficient to allow for the following: fresh sea air, silence, and a wide open space for the bits and pieces of my remains to stretch out on.

Elizabeth slept through the flight. I stroked her head for a while, feeling the softness of her curls.

CHAPTER
SEVEN

I arrived with Greta at the Port of Halifax on September 24, 1954, on the SS *Dundee*. I remember feeling such hope and such relief. I was free of that fear of detection, of arrest, and worse. Krasnodar and Mariupol were far behind. Germany, too, was gone. We'd chosen, Greta and I, to escape that old world, the incarcerating shadows of our past, and so the immediacy of events of the present extinguished my fears and my regrets and my shame. Memory was a stain that remained hidden.

We had been sponsored by an association of German Mennonite families living in Kitchener. It did not matter that I was not Mennonite. They simply wanted to assist us. They helped us find an apartment, and they helped me obtain my first job. I began work at an architect's firm and they were impressed with my education and my talent for drafting, drawing blueprints to bring order into the world, and with my eagerness to work. In the evenings I studied English and did my best to teach Greta to speak English, too. It was very difficult for her at first. She told me that she did not have my skill at learning and remembering all those words and phrases; she despaired of ever learning English and she was terribly homesick. I told her it would take time, and I was very patient with her. Every day I told her that I loved her, and that made her try harder. Soon she could converse in English with veritable ease, though her accent never lost its depth and harshness to an English ear.

In those first few years it was difficult, but it was like that for everyone like us. Eventually we prospered, and purchased a small home. Later I was offered a very advantageous position with an architectural firm in Winnipeg. We left Kitchener and bought a large stone-and-brick house in Winnipeg on Elm Street. It had a long, wide yard, and we made plans for a garden and for shrubs and trees and flowers. Winnipeg became our home. We continued to prosper and we melded into the fabric of that society, and I thought that the past, my past, had been put behind me.

Greta learned that she could not have children. This saddened us, but did nothing to rupture or weaken our bond. It made us cling to one another, because we knew in this world we would only ever have one another. I told her that she had been my saviour, and that she had rescued me and brought light and love to my life, and that she could not fathom how dark and pointless life had seemed to me in the moments before she came into my life. She told me that there was a

time, before Stalingrad, when her first husband had come to
Berlin on leave and they had spent two weeks together. She
said that she could see how the war had changed him. It was
in his eyes. There was such a sadness about him, and something else too, she said. Behind his eyes she could see a kind
of blackness, like a void. After those two weeks he was sent
back to the East and she never saw him again. He vanished
in the ruins of Stalingrad. She told me that when we met in
Marburg she saw in my eyes that same void, that nothingness,
and it horrified her. It was the void, the nothingness, that
made us flee Germany. On the ss *Dundee* I promised her
that I would never stop loving her, and she said that it was
then that the darkness left my eyes.

Another envelope arrived this morning. It was like the others,
bearing a postmark from Ottawa but no return address. This
one contained several typed pages and it looked very official,
like an excerpt from some kind of a report. I let the papers fall
out of the envelope one by one onto my kitchen table. I saw
Richmaier's name. The papers said that he'd been captured by
the Soviets. They also said that I had been a killer. That I had
stood at the edge of the parapet shooting down into the
bodies. There was another name, too, a name I had forgotten
until I saw it again, typed out in that report. *Sikorenko.* When
I saw that name his face appeared in my mind's eye. He had
the face of a fox. Narrow eyes. I was flung again back into the
past, my past. I pronounced his name out loud and I lingered
on each syllable as I let it glide across my dry lips. I ran my
finger across the paper, across the typed names. Sounds and

smells and sights seemed to fly up from those pages all at once, like an invisible current that ran through my fingertips and caused my heart to race.

My eyes were open, but I saw nothing but my own thoughts, and those sights held me for a moment in a deep and dark place; I felt the old terror surge up again. I felt the paralysis of that fear, at once enervating and absorbing.

I believed at that moment that my fate lay with Sikorenko's.

He knew. He had been there, and if they knew him, they knew me. They would know the truth of me. I heard his name when we were still in Rostov. That was when I first laid eyes upon the man. I was told that he was a Russian, one of Fedorov's men. He'd joined the kommando shortly before we arrived in Rostov and he was with the unit when we were based in Krasnodar. Whether he had volunteered or been drummed into service, I do not know. But he came to know me.

There was a time that I remember when I had been at the edge of a trench staring down at the bodies, watching as the steam rose from their wounds, finishing off the survivors. I looked back and this stranger was standing there, with a line of shooters, a few yards behind me. He was staring at me, and though he was older than I was, I thought that he looked so much like a child. His hands were shaking and I could see that this must have been the first time that he had had to perform such duties. And I felt a kind of contempt for him because he seemed so weak and fragile, and all because he had shot down a row of Jews for the very first time. I might have looked just like that when it was my first time, but that

was irrelevant now because so many killings had altered me
and hardened me. I realized then that the only thing that
concerned me was that the rest of the *Aktion* be completed
so that I could go back to the barracks and drink schnapps
and joke with Holtzmann and Nachtigal and dream of a time
when the war would be over and there would be no more
Aktionen and I would be rid of this godforsaken place.

Now my hands shook, and I felt a terror, a nausea, build
within me as I read this further fragment, this further dark
chapter of my past.

English Translation of the Statement of
Anatoliy Sikorenko

(Obtained by KGB *investigators October 6, 1962)*

. . . I served with the German punitive organ named
EK10A. I was with the unit in the regions of Krasnodar
and Novorossijsk. I knew the interpreters Penner, Fast,
and Reile. On many occasions I saw Reile participating
in the executions of Russian civilians.

In Krasnodar, Reile assisted in the loading of persons
from the cellar of the EK headquarters into the backs of
the gas trucks. I personally observed these actions on
many occasions. . . .

. . . On one occasion we were ordered by the
Commander Christmann to accompany the gas trucks to
the psychiatric hospital near Krasnodar. Reile and the
interpreter Penner translated orders of the German
officers who attended to the hospital. I saw Skripkin and
Psarev and others force the patients into the backs of the

gas trucks. Though I observed these actions I did not actually force any of the patients into the trucks. . . .

. . . In September or October 1943, part of the kommando was sent to Jejsk to arrest and interrogate suspected commissars and partisans. Jews were also collected and shot at pits located outside the city near an airstrip. I guarded the perimeter at such actions, but I was able to observe the interpreters participate in the shootings. I saw the interpreter Reile shoot Jewish victims with a machine gun and a pistol. . . .

During an action at Gaiduk near Novorossijsk, I was present with other members of the kommando and observed the interpreter Reile order Jewish citizens to undress and leave their valuables in a large crate. Groups of ten Jews were selected and shot into a large pit.

I personally know that the interpreter Reile was responsible for the shooting of a young woman who was forced to work as a cook at the kommando headquarters in Krasnodar. On Christmas Eve, 1942, I was ordered by Reile to take the young woman from the kitchen and put her into a kommando truck that was parked in the courtyard behind the headquarters. . . .

The young woman pleaded with me to let her go, but to do so would have meant I would have been shot.

Reile drove the truck to a place outside of the city near an electrical plant. The young girl was ordered out of the truck and forced to kneel beside a ditch. Reile shot her with his pistol. He then ordered me to cover her body with snow and we returned to the headquarters. I drove back in the front of the truck with Reile. He told me that I had to keep my mouth shut about this. He said that one of the German officers, named Goertzen, had ordered Reile to have the woman shot. . . .

That girl. I had made myself forget that girl. She worked in the kitchen at the kommando headquarters in Krasnodar. She was Russian. Her name was Tatiana and she was slight and dark, with a fine nose and dark eyes. She always wore a kerchief to keep her hair tied back when she worked. I began to weep as the memory of that event suddenly descended upon me. I had willed myself to forget her. I held my head in my hands and let the papers drop to the floor. I wept like a child, the agony of that memory ripping through me as if rending my soul.

I remember that horse doctor, Goertzen, his pig face, drunk, swearing about that whore. He could be shot, he said, he could be arrested. He said, "You must shoot that whore." Pig eyes, pig face. He said that she had given him a venereal disease. He told me to take her out of the city and shoot her. I told him that she was not Jewish, but that simply made him hysterical. He was frightened, he told me. "Shoot her tonight, before anyone finds out about this."

Christmas Eve, of all nights. While the kommando men celebrated in the mess hall, I took her from the kitchen and down to the courtyard where a kommando truck was parked. She had worked at the headquarters long enough to know what this meant. She cried and pleaded with me. But it was no use. I had no choice. I believed I had no choice. I ordered Sikorenko to sit with her so she would not try to escape. She was trembling and looked very tiny in the back of that truck. I threw a shovel into the back, which fell near her, and she shrieked when she saw it. Sikorenko slapped her into silence.

I drove to the electrical plant and ordered her out of the truck. I told her to kneel beside a deep ditch. She was silent now, her eyes wide, filled with terror. I told her it would be very quick. She knelt and I moved her head forward slightly. I felt the fabric of her kerchief, soft, brightly coloured. Then I fired into the base of her neck and she was flung forward by the blast. Sikorenko laughed, joking about the way she now lay in the ditch, sprawled out, the blood streaming from her head. I swung my pistol about and jammed the barrel into his forehead. He was silent then. I would have shot him. I should have shot him. But I hesitated, and my anger subsided. I left him to cover the body with snow and I drove away in the truck back to the headquarters. As I walked down the hall to my bunk I heard a gramophone playing "Stille Nacht."

I look at my hands that shake so. I see my old hands . . . and I see the hands that held the pistol, that pushed the young woman's head forward a little so it would be quicker.

I see the hands of a monster.

The last page in the envelope was titled "Assessment of the Reile Case." I let my eyes run down the words. What difference could this make now?

... According to the statement of Sikorenko ... other statements ... former kommando members ... clearly proven that Reile was a member of the Einsatzkommando 10A ... he took an active part in killing operations ... kommando members have stated that there was an unwritten standing order that all members of the unit would have to participate in at least one execution ... remembered that the size of EK10A never likely exceeded 130 men at any given time ... covering a very large area ... during the shooting operations ... large-scale ... all members of the unit ... had to participate. ...

... The interpreters were needed by the German kommando members to translate orders for the Russian Collaborator Units (HiWis) and Ukrainian Police Units ... communicate orders ... the Jews ... executions. ...

A review of all the documentary evidence and the witness statements establishes that Reile played a significant part in many of the mass executions carried out by EK10A. A recommendation should be made to indict the suspect ...

I felt as if I were being consumed by a dream; these horrors, these terrors — all of them were a dream. The envelopes, the letters, the words, the fragments, the story of all those things, those places, those names, lie before me now folded into the covers of the diary, along with my words written out in my hand, not memories any more, but part of the present. It is for them, when they come to take me, for the men in uniforms or in raincoats, like the ones the detectives wear on television.

It all happened, because it was now written down, recorded on these pages. It was no dream. Dreams serve to allow us an escape, and these things were too horrid to be the stuff of dreams. They bore all the hallmarks of real life. And yet, and yet . . . I still could not see me. I had been there, but I could not *see* me there, among them, as if all the things were acts that I observed from a distance . . . and yet it was me. I stood beside Christmann and Nachtigal and Holtzmann. I drove in the truck with Richmaier, and I obeyed Goertzen. . . . I put the pistol to the back of her head . . . And yet . . .

I was resigned now to await my judgement. I would await the punishment, the retribution, the reckoning that I must surely have to endure. The photos, the statements, the confessions, all those words; surely there was proof enough. And when I knew that they would come I felt a kind of resolution. I sat in my study at the front of my house, sipping schnapps and thinking again of Mariupol and Krasnodar and the acrid smell of smoke and blood and the sharp coldness of the sound of gunfire that no amount of time could obliterate.

CHAPTER
EIGHT

I

Elizabeth returned to Toronto in March 1994. This came as no surprise. We both knew that she had to leave. She wanted to go back to her old office, where she felt she could accomplish something. I understood her sentiments. We continued our relationship until the day that she departed. We had talked about what would happen once she moved back. I had to stay in Ottawa and she had to stay in Toronto. There was no getting around that simple fact. Even from a practical viewpoint, neither of us was in a position to simply quit our job in the hopes of finding a new one in a new city. We agreed it would be too hard to maintain any sort of intimacy if the only way it could be preserved was through long-distance telephone calls and monthly weekend visits. We agreed to part, not without sadness, not without suffering from the sense of loss, but in recognition of the simple fact that sometimes people just leave. She had to go. She had served her sentence. That was the deal.

That first morning after she left, I woke up early and sat in front of the tiny screen of my television for hours, transfixed and sedated, my mind partially anesthetized. I flipped incessantly between channels, sometimes so quickly that the screen resembled a strobe. Forty channels in all; but forty times zero is still zero. I hovered around each channel, sometimes for a second, sometimes several minutes, and then fled: I hovered and fled over and over and watched through a tiny window as the events of the world unfolded in sound-bites and clips until everything was repeated and nothing was ever really said, and meaning was lost in images and sound.

I spent the whole day there, in front of the television, watching everything and nothing. There was a tremendous hole in my life. That night I dreamed of her eyes. They were blue and bright and I thought I heard her voice as I awoke, but it was just part of the dream. I felt an almost intolerable sadness that second day without her. It was only then that I finally realized she had gone. It left me pained, but it also left me beginning to feel very cold inside.

II

In retrospect I would have to say that the death of Sikorenko probably heralded the beginning of the end for the unit. It was generally accepted that the Reile file was the best thing we had going at the moment in the way of a triable case. There was no question that further steps would be required to put the case in better shape. More document searches, perhaps more interview trips, but Sikorenko would have been the centrepiece of the trial. He could have fingered Reile right in that courtroom and I would have been there to see it happen. And maybe Elizabeth would have been brought back to assist with the prosecution. Maybe a thousand other things would have happened to improve the quality of my life and bring some kind of a smile to my face. But nothing like that happened, because nothing like that ever does. Instead, Sikorenko was dead, the case was now a bust, and that left a kind of vacuum that was not about to be filled. In the months that followed, each team of lawyers and historians pursued their files and went off with the police investigators on yet another witness-interview trip, but the clock was ticking.

I continued working on other files, preparing more

reports, reviewing old documents, compiling more lists of names. I still chatted with Viaux and went for afternoon strolls with Digby. His life was not going well at the time, being decidedly still in the shitter, or in close proximity to it. Bryndyce had not taken his infidelity lightly. After initially banishing him from the marital homestead she had let him return for a few months to attempt a reconciliation.

"I don't know what she had in mind," he told me, "but it certainly was not reconciliation." Instead, as Digby described it, "She used it as an opportunity to abuse me, torture me, harangue me, and otherwise make my life miserable every second of the day I was in her presence. She said that she had to work out her anger before we could move on. I saw a lot of anger but not much progress. In fact, I began to suspect she was rather enjoying it all."

I was not surprised. I thought of Bryndyce's mean little eyes, that pouty little chin. Life with Digby was probably much more pleasant for her now that she had something on him and therefore, as the victim of his infidelity, had an excuse to be spiteful and cruel.

In April 1994 I went to Munich for a month to review some additional trial records and documents relating to the Christmann trial. A couple of years earlier, I had skimmed over these documents while searching for information relevant to the Reile file, but I did not copy them as none of it related to Reile. Since that time, new files had been opened concerning two more ethnic German interpreters. We had very little in the way of background information, not even knowing for sure what units they served with, but I proposed to Goreman that I go back to Munich to see if the trial records contained any reference to either suspect. He exhibited little enthusiasm, but authorized the trip.

I found nothing that might assist either case and flew back to Canada at the end of the four weeks. The flight home brought back memories. I couldn't help but think of Elizabeth again and the trip we had taken to Moscow. It was perverse, silly, but every aspect of international travel somehow reminded me of her. I sat scrunched up for hours in economy class on the flight from Frankfurt to Toronto glumly contemplating our past, feeling quite lonely, wondering if I should call her. We had decided that this might not be a good thing, at least for the first few months. It would be too hard. I agreed. We had so many agreements like that, level-headed, sensible understandings and protocols. We had more agreements on breaking up than we did on being together.

Other than finding myself plunged into a black funk over Elizabeth and life generally, it was an average, uneventful flight. That is to say the airplane was packed with tourists, the overhead storage bins were filled to capacity, with no room for my carry-on luggage, which meant that I had to stuff it under the seat in front of me, leaving little leg room, so that my knees were bent and throbbing throughout the long flight. It was warm and stuffy and the meal flung at me by an indifferent stewardess was inedible (I'd call them "attendants" the moment I saw one of them actually *attend*). After dinner, all the stewardesses fled to what I imagined was a secret and spacious location on the airplane where they could hide from the rabble for a few hours and avoid troublemakers such as myself who had the temerity to order a second, thimble-sized, five-buck glass of plonk, and attempt to pay with a ten-dollar bill instead of the exact change.

III

The end came on the Friday of the third week of December 1994. I was the last man. I was the one that had to turn off the lights on the way out, literally. There was nothing more to be done. I had planned to send another excerpt to Reile but there was no more time, and it seemed to me now that the effort might be redundant. In my mail campaign I had done what I could. I could not have been more specific. That last envelope, with the statement from the late Sikorenko, should have done it. There would have been nothing else to say.

On the day that the SPU officially closed down, I left in the late afternoon. The last secretary had left the day before, all the files now having been properly closed. I had only returned to pack my books and papers into several boxes. It took several trips up and down the elevator but eventually I loaded the lot into the trunk and back seat of the car I'd rented for this very job. I went back up to the sixth floor one more time. I took a last stroll along that hallway, past every office, every room, every nook and cranny and crevice and space and corner. I had one last cup of coffee, settling for instant, and a cigarette in the coffee room. Then I walked out the main entrance on the sixth floor, leaving the keys inside on the front desk where a security guard had once sat, and where I assumed someone might collect them. The door locked automatically behind me as I left. I rode down the elevator and out a delivery door at the rear of the building where my car was parked.

I left behind that beige mausoleum and did not look up at the windows of the sixth floor as I drove away. I wondered if there were any ghosts left behind, peering out, locked away now and forgotten. Probably not; even ghosts have to move along from time to time.

It turned out that I did have a place to go, after all. I learned this barely two days before my employment with the SPU was to be terminated. I had received a letter from the Acting Director of the Regional Office of the Historical Research Branch, Contemporary Studies Section of the Directorate of Foreign Matters in Toronto (the A/D, ROHRB (CSS), DOFM, for short). It was a two-year-term position, likely to be renewed. It was not clear from the letter what I was expected to do. Neither was it clear to me what it was that the ROHRB etc. actually *did*. Nevertheless, the rate of pay was relatively generous. They'd pay to move me, and I could start whenever I wanted.

Apparently the acting director had heard good things about me. I read the letter and read between the lines. Goreman had done me a favour. He had sent a glowing letter to the headquarters of the Directorate of Foreign Matters in Ottawa, a few blocks away, commending me for my long and dedicated service to the SPU and recommending that I be

considered as a candidate for any available employment positions. Normally that type of glowing letter means you've
been fired, or worse, but this one was considered an exception. They actually *wanted* to hire me. I was a bit surprised at
Goreman's largesse. At the SPU we were never close, and we
were obviously never close in any sense of physical proximity, since he never seemed to be in the office.

Then it occurred to me why he might want to do me a
favour. It was as I told Digby. I was burying all the bodies,
disposing of the evidence, and dumping the remains offshore.
I made it all go away with little fuss and less muss. Perhaps he
was grateful. But it wasn't his style, really, to express any form
of gratitude. Maybe he just thought I had something on him,
and this would keep me quiet, since I would now owe him.

On another day I might have been offended, but beggars
can't be choosers and scrupulous integrity doesn't bring
home a paycheque. I called the acting director in Toronto
and accepted his offer. I told him I could start the first week
of January and sent a letter to confirm the acceptance. That
would give me time to close the last file, in person.

I telephoned my mother the week before Christmas and told
her I was planning to be home in Winnipeg for the holidays.
Delighted, she said this was a wonderful surprise, since I had
not been home for Christmas in five years. She asked me if
there was anything special that I wanted for Christmas this
year, and I told her I had everything that I needed, so she
should not go to any trouble.

I arrived in Winnipeg three days before Christmas. My mother had wanted to meet me at the airport, but she was concerned that she would have to drive in the dark and that there might be a difficulty parking her car. I told her that I would catch a taxi. I collected my luggage at the carousel, loaded it onto a cart, and exited the terminal to be met by a wall of biting, bitter, unforgivingly cold air. *But it's a dry cold*, I was often told when I lived there, by many an adoring denizen of this city, who could not bear even a hint of criticism. *And we have the most days of sunshine in the country, even in the winter.* Fine, I'd think, but, you see, forty below zero is still forty below zero, so with that in mind I didn't care how fucking sunny it might be outside, the cold and snow were still intolerable. I quickly flung myself and my luggage into a taxi.

Fifteen minutes later, the taxi pulled up to the front door of my mother's home on Waterloo. The curbs on either side of the street were piled high with snow, but the street was quite cheerful, as most of the houses had Christmas lights or decorations of some sort hanging on the insides and outsides of their windows and doors. My mother's house was likewise decorated on the outside with a string of red, green, and yellow lights that flickered and flashed on and off.

My mother was happy to see me, she claimed, and gave me a peck on the cheek as I struggled through the door with my bags. She seemed smaller now, but otherwise unchanged. Once I'd taken my coat off and dumped my bags in my old room I joined her in the living room to marvel at her decorating acumen. There were lights and tinsel and baubles and little miniature Yuletide scenes in every imaginable space and corner.

She was particularly proud of the Christmas "tree." I was asked to admire the manner in which she had flung great clingy globs of tinsel onto the thick bundles of white nylon needles wrapped about the wire of each artificial branch. Any real tree would have collapsed beneath the weight of the several strings of multicoloured lights wrapped about the tree like a series of nooses. An eclectic mix of plastic ornaments, frosted tin bells, mini-Santas and reindeer were strung at haphazard angles. I suspected that a few generous portions of sweet sherry had preceded her decorating efforts.

I excused myself for a moment after assuring her that the effect indeed was enchanting and magical. I went down the hall and used the washroom. Walking past the study I noted that it, too, was full of lights, tinsel, and a miniature version of the tree in the living room. I paused for a moment in my old room and then returned to the living room where my mother was seated. This had been the house of my youth and my teenage years, and it had changed very little since the day I left to go east to university and then to work. But it was no longer my home, and I sensed that nothing of me had survived within its walls.

My father had died several years before, and having survived the initial shock of that loss my mother had readily managed to fill that vacancy. She became accustomed to being alone, and indeed she became quite self-sufficient, more so than when my father had been alive and had catered to her every need. My father had scrimped and saved and done without all his life, and he'd invested wisely; in doing so he had conceived an ample nest egg for the two of them, to be shared on the occasion of his retirement and thereafter. He obliged her further by joining the Hereafter, dying barely a year after he retired. The ample nest egg for two became a windfall for one.

My father had spent the last twenty years of his life dreaming of his retirement, as if it heralded some form of great emancipation. As a teenager I remember sitting at the dinner table listening to him talk about all the plans he had in mind once that blessed day arrived. There were the trips he and my mother would take to places like Egypt and France and Hawaii. He said that he would go golfing every morning and read all those books that he had always wanted to read. And there were all those other projects too, like building model sailing ships and maybe taking a night course or two at the university.

None of that came to pass. Within weeks of his retirement I watched as he became increasingly distracted, as if he had begun to unravel. He would tell me he just felt like he was at loose ends. He took a stab at golfing a few times a week and he did go out and buy that elaborate model sailing ship kit. He went to bookstores too and began to tackle all of those books he always thought he ought to read. He did *try* to get started, but he seemed to lack inspiration. He never finished any of the books he started, and the model sailing ship still sat in a corner of the basement of my mother's house. He'd bought all the tools and paints and special glue. He'd opened the box and carefully read the instructions, and he glued and painted some of the plastic pieces to construct the hull. But for some reason he never got beyond that. A kind of lethargy crept into his body and soul. I saw him age before me in those months of his retirement. He had worked for forty years for this moment and now that it was here he could not handle the lack of structure and direction.

In the last month of his life, just before I left to go to university, he literally began to fade away. He had a stroke, which left him partly paralyzed and unable to speak. My mother cared for him at home for a while, or rather looked on as a series of home-care workers and nurses visited in shifts to look after my father. I would fly home when I could to watch him fade. It was too hectic, though, given all the medical personnel and equipment regularly present in the house, so my visits were usually short. My father was so changed by his condition, I did not recognize him slumped on the bed. While I was gone he had another stroke and was too ill to remain at home. He died in the hospital a few days later. I made it home for the funeral, and when it was over my mother complained generally about incompetent doctors, how much work it had been to care for my father, and how thoughtless and noisy the care-workers and nurses had been. After his death, my mother and I rarely spoke, and I stopped going home for Christmas. This was not a gesture designed to hurt, nor a statement. There just seemed to be no point to my going back, Christmas or not. Until now.

In contrast to my father, my mother at sixty-five years of age remained vital, independent, and incorrigibly self-centred. She recovered from the shock of losing her husband and quietly resolved to get on with her remaining years. Some kind of inner strength emerged at the time of her loss and it now propelled her through life. At its source that strength seemed to foster an assured conclusion that she was indeed the only person that still mattered on this earth. She knew very little about what I did for a living except that I "hunted old Nazis" and she didn't require any further information in that regard since it had no immediate impact on her life. On the rare occasions we spoke on the telephone (Sunday afternoons, when the long-distance rates were cheaper) she would ask me how my work was going, or rather she would tell me that it must be going well.

"You like your work," she'd say to me, in a high squeaky tone, which I think was her manner of asking me a question and then including what she assumed would be my reply, without the necessity of actually having to hear from me on the subject. This permitted her to deftly return to the meaningful concerns of her own sphere of interest.

I would say, "Work's fine, I guess, except it looks like they might be closing down the office and . . ."

But I would advance no further than that because she would then embark on some other track altogether.

"Your father worked in a big office like yours in Ottawa and so did I but *I* had to quit when we were married. . . . Those were different days back then. . . . Your mother was very smart, you know. . . . I would have been a real higher-up then if I could have stayed on. But I had to leave because I married your father. That wouldn't happen today. Women don't want to quit their jobs and raise a family like your mother did. They just want to shove them in daycare. Oh well. I looked after your father, you know, when he was sick. There's not a lot of people that would do the same for your mother. Not these days. It's everyone for themselves. That's the way it is. . . . I should have been Mother of the Year. . . . There's not much else new to tell you, though. That crack in the basement foundation really concerns me. I have to get a man in to look at it again. I can't trust them, though. They're all lazy. In the spring there'll be reams of water and that carpet will be ruined. It's the city's fault, you know. We pay all these taxes and they won't even clear the snow on time and I pay those two lads to clear the snow from the walkway but they don't do a great job. They leave patches of snow. I darn near killed myself walking to the car. My remote starter's on the fritz, too, and I just bought it so the warranty must still be good. But my car's in good shape. . . ."

We spent Christmas Day together, just the two of us. I received a number of silly, rather odd gifts, in spite of the fact that I had asked her not to buy me anything. She had not listened to my suggestion that we not exchange gifts, and so I unwrapped a series of softcover copies of books that she had already given to me once, and "knickknacks" for my apartment, and stainless-steel pickle trays, and an assortment of junky items that she liked to call "just little things," along with an assortment of items she had cleared out of her basement. She abhorred clutter, and seemed obsessed with ridding the house of any and all of those items that had accumulated in her basement in the years of her marriage.

For years now she had been trying to get me to take all my LPs out of my old room. It never occurred to her that I could not possibly carry two hundred records in a suitcase with the rest of my luggage and board an airplane back to Ottawa. (For some reason she felt that I might be attached to such things for sentimental reasons that I could not fathom. It was, after all, truly nothing but junk.)

Over dinner our conversations centred once again around the crack she'd discovered in the foundation of her house, the rust-proofing in her new car, her trips to Hawaii and Spain, critical observations on her nosy, or unfriendly, or inconsiderate neighbours, whom she thoroughly detested, her suspicions concerning the man she'd paid to shovel her walkway in winter and cut her lawn in summer.... It went on and on like this, without cease. There was no responding to any one thing she said since she provided little opportunity for interjection or reactive conversation. Her utterances were one long and meandering diatribe, and any interjections on my part were restricted to "Uh-huh" and "I see" and sometimes, for variety, "Oh really?" and "Is that so?" I drank heavily through this discourse, as did she. My poison was wine, but I soon moved on to the single-malt Scotch held in copious amounts in her liquor cabinet, having remained untouched since the demise of my father. She, more restrained than I, restricted herself to an uninterrupted and inebriative flow of sherry and port.

After dinner we cleaned up the dishes and retired to the living room. She carried on talking and I continued to drink. Towards the end of the evening she stumbled as she approached the Christmas tree, trying to point out a favourite ornament that she had loved, or my father had loved, or someone had loved, and she fell headfirst into that unkempt and faux-arboreal erection, festooned as it was with lights and tinsel and plastic globs and wires of all sorts. With her ignominious descent I knew that Christmas Day and Christmas Night were at an end, and so I helped her up and to bed. Just before I left her she told me that she loved me, and that she missed my father so, and that he had been so good to her; and I caught from her breath the whiff of a good many doses of fortified wine. I said that he must have loved her and that I loved her, too, and I thanked her for a wonderful Christmas. Then I let my dry and pale lips press against her papery cheeks for a brief moment. But I drew my lips back just as quickly and never let on how the sight of her and the touch of her was so repellent to me, how the words that I uttered, the words that I let pass, the words "I love you, too" were shed as a mere fluctuation of the muscles of my throat. Though effortless, these words were forced and fraudulent, the extortion of some exterior force that said I had to feel love in spite of the fact that I never did.

Assured that she'd gone to sleep. I went into action, albeit well-fortified with the effervescence of too much wine and Scotch. I drove my mother's well-preserved and spotless car to a convenience store. Christmas Day or not, it was open for business, and I bought two dozen eggs. It was only about two kilometres to *his* house, but I took an indirect route, avoiding main roads, skirting back and forth along side streets and back alleys. Being decidedly pissed I wished to avoid any police check-stops erected for the purpose of detecting or deterring precisely this kind of activity.

I drove past the house, but the lights were out. It was quite large, three storeys, and constructed of grey brick. I knew he was there, since I'd called his home a couple of times earlier that day and hung up both times when he answered. I recognized his voice. It was the voice I had heard a few weeks before when I'd called pretending to update his tax file, the voice that told me he was German, not Irish.

The wine and the Scotch had made me reckless, and the new concept of a call-display device revealing my mother's number neither occurred to me nor deterred me. I simply did not care. I drove by his house, then parked a block away and walked back along an alleyway to his house. The numbness of my drunken state served to insulate me from the cold. I stumbled a bit on the icy road and at one point slipped and fell. I was carrying the cartons of eggs in a plastic bag which flew into the air and landed on a snowbank. I swore and checked both cartons but the eggs remained intact. For the first time in my life I was grateful for the presence of so much snow.

My hip ached where I had fallen, but I continued walking to the end of the alley. I was at the rear of his house. There was a high wooden fence all around so I could not see in. I came out of the alley and walked along the sidewalk that led to his street. I turned to the left and found myself a few yards from his doorstep. I saw the black metal mailbox beside the door, the ultimate destination of my correspondence.

I put the plastic bag down, took off my gloves and stuffed them into the pockets of my coat. Then I removed the first carton of eggs from the bag. I looked to the left and to the right. The street was empty, and though most of the houses still had their Christmas lights on, the houses were otherwise dark. His house likewise appeared dark inside, just a string of white lights hung on an evergreen to the right of his door.

The Styrofoam carton squeaked a little as I opened it. I began flinging eggs, two at a time. The first two were wildly off target. One missed the house altogether, the other one fell harmlessly through the branches of the evergreen. But I found my range and my precision improved. I aimed for the large picture window at the front and the smaller one a little over to the left. I flung the eggs with as much force and energy as I could, relishing the satisfying smacks as they collided with the glass. They exploded into a gooey mass that ran a bit, but otherwise remained stuck to the point of impact.

When I'd exhausted my supply I threw the two Styrofoam containers aside and reached into my coat to remove one more envelope. I couldn't see where the walkway to his front door began, so I tried to take a shortcut across his yard. The snow was much deeper than it appeared, and I found myself knee-deep in the stuff. I stumbled and fell, my hands submerged into the icy whiteness. I struggled to get up, finally finding my way to the walkway. I tramped up to his door. I raised my fist to pound on the door, then hesitated. Perhaps the cold and the adrenaline had sobered me up a little, allowing for a moment of reflection and the intervention of a bit of common sense. I didn't want to see him, not like this. Not when I could barely talk, or even form a sentence.

I took the envelope, opened the lid of his mailbox, and stuffed it into the box. *Fucker.* I swore to myself and then walked back down the front steps, this time using the walkway that led to the sidewalk beside his street. As I followed the sidewalk back around to the alley, I noticed that the house was still dark. I was weaving a little now and felt very tired. I must have gone a block too far because I could not find my car. I swore in frustration and pain, since I really felt the cold now, and my coat did little to protect me. After stumbling around for several minutes I finally found the car. I had lost my gloves somehow, and my fingers were stiff and numb, even though I had stuffed them into my coat pockets. I fumbled with the keys, but managed to unlock the door and get in. I let the car run a few minutes while I warmed up, then I drove home, one eye shut so I could focus.

At home I sat in a chair in the living room, drunk, sad, full of self-pity. Then I began to weep. These were the kinds of sobs that only liquor could rend from me. I wept silently so my mother would not hear. I went to sleep after that but woke up early in the morning. My mouth was dry and sour and my heart was racing.

Then I remembered what I had done. I thought of going back there, to confront him on his own doorstep, but that had never been part of the plan. There seemed to be no point. It was too late. That was the best that I could do.

IV

She met me at the airport in Toronto beside the luggage turnstile and greeted me with a kind of sad smile. She put her arms around me for a few seconds. Her hair was longer, a different cut. She was dressed up, with a blue coat that seemed somehow too big for her. She looked thinner, perhaps too thin. I held her and felt the warmth of her while crowds of people milled about. I smelled her perfume, *lemons and limes*, and it took me back for a moment to that sixth floor, to the darkened offices and the empty beige hallway, the wall-to-wall and the endless piles of papers left behind, in darkness and in silence, when files were closed and locked away.

CHAPTER NINE

December 26, 1994.

My life is a continuum: smoke; soil; frost; the whiteness of newly fallen snow; my breath in the morning air at Mariupol. The crackle of gunfire in cold, clear air.

There is a clarity borne of coldness. There is memory. There are shadows. And sometimes I see in those shadows of dreams the white froth absorbed by a blue and black sea.

I heard him last night. I heard the missiles being flung at the window and the door. I thought they were bullets at first, smacking against the frost-laden glass. I sat in my room watching the first missiles strike the window. But the glass did not break and I thought perhaps they were snowballs flung by children, vandals playing pranks. But then the noise did not abate, and I imagined that the snowballs had become rocks or perhaps bullets again. Then there was silence and I heard the metallic, squeaky sound of my mailbox being opened and closed. I knew then that it must have been him.

I lay awake the rest of that night staring up at that window, feeling that this was my last night on earth. I waited, and I watched, and when the light filtered through my window I rose. I lacked the strength to go to my door, and it was not until just before noon that I summoned the courage to look into the mailbox.

There was a piece of paper, folded and a little crumpled because it had been stuffed into my mailbox. In the centre of the page a sentence had been scrawled out in longhand. It was written in blue ink:

Richmaier's dead. Sikorenko's dead. They're all dead. So now you're off the hook, but one day you'll be dead, too. It's over. You should never have lived this long.

I looked up and down the street but there was no one. I read the note again and then folded it. I walked into my study, shivering a bit from the cold. I placed the piece of paper at the last page of my diary.

Later in the afternoon I donned a heavy coat and went outside. I scraped the remains of the frozen eggs and shells from the front windows of my house. The embryos had crystallized in the bitter cold and were now easy to remove. I looked about and saw that the sky was cloudless, pale and blue, and the sun shone brightly though it lay low in the afternoon sky. On either side the sun had its doppelgängers, sundogs they're called, mirrors of the light suspended in the sky. Long, narrow shadows stretched away from lampposts and trees, extending across the thick layers of snow that covered the front yard of my home.

I paused in that fading daylight and watched for a while as the sky turned from pale blue to grey and then began to darken and the shades and hues of the sky began to meld into one. I exhaled and watched my white breath ascend and fade and then disappear into the night until there was nothing left of it that I could see. Silence. My breath rose into and through the night sky, and all that remained was that silence and the emptiness of the cold air. And no one came because no one ever would, and I was left with the blankness of that night and the coldness that would endure, forever, like an eternal emptiness.

After I had retired and while Greta was still alive we spent the winter months in warm places like Miami Beach, as well as California and Mexico. We never went overseas, to Europe, to Germany. I feared for my safety there, though I never shared these thoughts with Greta. After the trials in Munich I *knew* that I could never go back to Germany. The clippings that my sister had sent me made it clear that many of the kommando men had escaped the Russians, escaped death, had survived the trials, and remained free and alive in Germany, for now. That was not a guarantee, though. I could not risk an encounter or detection. I could not risk seeing those faces, those men. Germany was split in two then, and there was perhaps the risk of being kidnapped by Soviet agents and taken to the East to be tried.

Greta had had no desire to return to Germany. She said that for people like us, Germany was a place that had ceased to exist, it was a place in our minds, bounded by our own thoughts and memories, some sweet, but others not so sweet, of the charnel house filled with all that was dreadful. It was better, she said, that we close the door of that house, and leave it behind. We never spoke of my service in Russia, and I wonder now if she did suspect, if she knew something of the part I played. But her love for me was such, perhaps, that she endeavoured to protect me from that past and from others who might want to hold me accountable.

In the last months of her life, when she was too sick to move, too sick to sit up, she would hold my hand as I sat beside her in the bedroom. Her grip would tighten with each spasm of pain and there was nothing that I could do. I watched her die. I watched the life slip out of her. I watched her eyes glaze over and become like marble, dead eyes that remained open and shiny in a pale reflection of life. Her last breath passed across my cheek and the warmth of it escaped her body, leaving nothing but the strangeness of silence in the midst of sound.

A few months after her death I travelled again to Miami Beach to stay at a hotel she had loved, in the room she had loved, the one that overlooked the beach and the Atlantic. That first night, after dinner, I walked for a while along the boardwalk that ran parallel to the beach and the sea. It was dark and warm and a breeze blew in from the sea. I was alone at first, moving slowly among the people going along the wooden walkway. They all seemed aged beyond their years, some hunched, moving slowly, shuffling. Others leaned heavily on canes or upon the supportive arms of the young men and women who helped them along their way, their daughters and sons perhaps. As I passed them I heard voices and snatches of conversations, and I listened to the varying tones of their soft, hoarse voices, still thickened by the accents of Eastern Europe. As I moved among them, through them, past them, they took no notice and they knew nothing of me. I was unknown, unseen. Simply another old man. Each night after that I walked along this same boardwalk. Each night I walked amongst them, like a ghost amongst the living, and they around me like the living unaware of a ghost.

One evening, before I was to return to Canada, I left the boardwalk and walked across the sand to the edge of the ocean. I stared out onto the water where the sea and the sky merged and became indistinguishable. Beyond there, on the water, were tiny points of light: ships moving through that blackness. Above, there were stars, clear then blurred, then clear again, constant then sporadic, then certain, then uncertain again. In between, though, there was no light, and only the sounds of waves and the wind. I could no longer hear the voices from the boardwalk, and there was nothing else that could be heard and nothing else that could be seen but points of tiny light in a sea of darkness.

Tonight I sat in my study again, as I had done before, sipping schnapps; but it was different now because a fire burned in the hearth and I was warm again. The past was gone, as if nothing had ever happened, and I was left alone again. I watched as the corners of the two photographs curled upwards in the flames, changing from white to black to glowing red, until they were consumed and reduced to ash.

AUTHOR'S NOTE

In Ottawa I worked for the War Crimes Unit, which operated under the direction of the Federal Department of Justice. The persons described in this novel as part of the "Special Prosecutions Unit" – a fictional group – bear no relation to anyone who worked at the War Crimes Unit.

By contrast, I am sorry to report that EKIOA did exist and did operate in the manner described in the regions of southern Ukraine, Rostov, and Krasnodar. Although I have used the surnames of some of those who actually served in the unit (Zeetzen, Christmann, Richmaier, Baumer, Fehr, Penner, Nachtigal, Trimborn, and Heimbach), the first names, the characters themselves, and the words they used, are products of my imagination.

ACKNOWLEDGEMENTS

I owe a great deal of thanks to the Manitoba Writer's Guild, Don Bailey, Patrick Friesen, Linda Holeman, Bridget Hoffer, and Elsa Franklin for their encouragement and enthusiasm. In addition, I wish to thank the Federal Department of Justice, and Douglas Gibson, Peter Buck, and the staff of McClelland & Stewart for their invaluable help and support.

I am indebted to the ever-patient Jack Hodgins, whose editing, advice, and counsel helped shape the novel into its finished form. I thank my parents-in-law, Dr. Henry and Elizabeth Dirks, for inspiring me with their acts of kindness and generosity.

And finally, I thank my wife, Janet, for her loyalty and love.